Toaru Majutsu no
Index Light Novel
Series

A Certain Magical

Index 3

KAZUMA KAMACHI

ILLUSTRATION BY
KIYOTAKA HAIMURA

"Chaser!"

Academy City Tokiwadai Middle School Student **Mikoto Misaka**

"...!!"

Academy City High School Student **Touma Kamijou**

"…!"

"…What is it? Misaka queries."

Mikoto's little sister **Misaka**

"Hah-hah! Why ya runnin' away? You tryin' to seduce
me by shakin' your ass all happy like that?!"

Academy City Level Five **Accelerator**

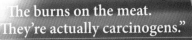

"The burns on the meat.
They're actually carcinogens."

Little Miss Shrine Maiden Freeloader **Aisa Himegami**

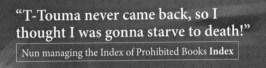

"T-Touma never came back, so I
thought I was gonna starve to death!"

Nun managing the Index of Prohibited Books **Index**

"I'm going to turn on the hot plate, okay?"

Touma Kamijou's homeroom teacher **Komoe Tsukuyomi**

contents

VOLUME 3

KAZUMA KAMACHI
ILLUSTRATION BY: KIYOTAKA HAIMURA

NEW YORK

A CERTAIN MAGICAL INDEX, Volume 3
KAZUMA KAMACHI

Translation by Andrew Prowse and Yoshito Hinton

This book is a work of fiction. Names, characters, places, and incidents are the product of the author's imagination or are used fictitiously. Any resemblance to actual events, locales, or persons, living or dead, is coincidental.

TOARU MAJYUTSU NO INDEX
©KAZUMA KAMACHI 2004
All rights reserved.
Edited by ASCII MEDIA WORKS
First published in 2004 by KADOKAWA CORPORATION, Tokyo.
English translation rights arranged with KADOKAWA CORPORATION, Tokyo,
through Tuttle-Mori Agency, Inc., Tokyo.

English translation © 2015 Hachette Book Group, Inc.

Yen On
Hachette Book Group
1290 Avenue of the Americas
New York, NY 10104

www.hachettebookgroup.com
www.yenpress.com

Yen On is an imprint of Hachette Book Group, Inc.
The Yen On name and logo are trademarks of Hachette Book Group, Inc.

The publisher is not responsible for websites (or their content) that are not owned by the publisher.

First Yen On edition: May 2015

ISBN: 978-0-316-34054-0

10 9 8 7 6 5 4 3 2 1

RRD-C

Printed in the United States of America

PROLOGUE

Radio Noise

Level2

The wind is strong.

It is twilight. A girl lies flat on her stomach, concealed on the roof of a building. Her eyes narrow slightly.

A mismatched rifle sits in her hands. No, it goes beyond the simple concept of being *mismatched*. The rifle, after all, is 184 centimeters in length. It is largely in excess of the girl's height.

The Metal-eater MX.

It is derived from the Bullet M82A1, an antitank rifle legendary for blowing up an armored car from two klicks away during the Okinawan War. They say that when it was created, it had such enormous recoil that it didn't need a full-automatic function. The Metal-eater, however, is an experimental type, onto which rapid-fire capabilities had been forced.

It is a brutal enough gun that its recoil alone could crush a flimsy helmet into tiny pieces. Somehow, however, the girl's slender body moves in perfect harmony with it. Impact is not something to be repressed but something to be accepted and redirected. By the end of her fourteen-day training via Testament, she could compute the shock released by the Metal-eater and calculate the most efficient means of redirecting it.

The girl holds her breath and stares down the cold, impersonal scope at her target, six hundred meters off.

Exiting a convenience store, lit up from within as if to attract gnats on this summer night, is a fifteen- or sixteen-year-old boy. His figure is as thin as a sewing needle, and white hair sits atop his feminine, delicate skin. He brings to mind the expression, "He'd blow away in a stiff wind."

Those who witnessed him would receive from him the impression of the tip of a knife. It's to be expected. The data banks spoke of his undefeated record in official combat, of course. However, he had never suffered even a glancing wound, nor had he ever blocked or avoided anything.

The concept of blocking an opponent's weapon is not a part of his existence. He is the incarnation of the sharp edge of a slim, narrow sword, forged to the extreme—its only objective is to rip through enemy flesh.

The girl does not know her target's true name. His code name is "Accelerator" or the "One-Way Road."

The young man who goes by this name stands at the pinnacle of the Level Five Superpowers, of which only seven reside in this single, great Ability Development agency with the moniker Academy City.

The crosswind is strong…Adjusting aim three klicks to the left, the girl says to herself, twisting the screw on the side of the scope.

The boy swinging the plastic bag from the store back and forth in boredom—he is her target.

If the girl was to confront Accelerator directly, she wouldn't stand a chance of winning. No, in all Academy City, there isn't a single opponent who could stand against Accelerator in a fair fight—or perhaps in even all the world.

On the other hand, that was all.

If you can't win in a fair fight, then don't pick one.

In the end, using supernatural abilities is no different from operating your arms and legs. As long as one isn't a Level Zero incredibly inexperienced at controlling their powers, their activation can be generally split into two varieties.

One is when the esper himself gives a command to use the power.

One is when the esper's body senses danger.

This makes things simple. Even espers were beatable as long as one didn't let on that they were attempting to kill one, then took his or her life with a single attack from the dark.

Originally, long-range sniping was a method used by Academy City's Judgment to arrest berserk espers. Though they used rubber bullets to end their consciousness, the girl will use armor-piercing rounds to end his life.

"Building winds...An eddy from three o'clock; adjusting aim one klick to the right," she said under her breath, making further adjustments to the scope.

Lead bullets actually blow around easily in the wind. On top of that, in spots with many buildings packed in close to one another, the wind doesn't blow in a simple line. It streams around the structures in various directions, and when the flows of air run into each other, they create eddies and scatter everywhere.

Missing was not an option. Her opponent was the strongest of the Level Fives. The moment her initial shot went astray, cluing him in to her ambush, would essentially be the very moment she was defeated—no matter how much distance separated them and no matter how far away she fled.

She places her finger on the trigger.

Her motions are without hesitation. Despite the fact that the boy at the end of her scope is human. Despite the fact that if she pulled this trigger, a .50 caliber antitank shell would rip through the air at twelve hundred kilometers per hour, altering the layout of his upper body at a speed faster than sound...Though logically she understands these ideas, there is not a trace of doubt on her face.

But one directive had been placed on her slight shoulders:

To destroy Accelerator, the most powerful Level Five, with a precise shot from the distance.

...

Her ears listen to the sounds of the wind. Eddies collide, and suddenly, the wind begins to glide in a single direction.

It would be for no more than two seconds. However, as soon as she is certain that the complex building winds have stabilized...

She pulls the trigger.

With a roar like a fireworks factory exploding, a handful of bullets tears through the air. Ridiculous as it may sound for a sharpshooter, she had actually fired on full auto. She forces herself to take the impact, which is heavy enough to topple a grown man. In the span of one second, she sends twelve shots down a path so precise it could thread a needle.

The girl ignores the fact that the cartridge had been emptied in just one second and tracks the fate of the boy in her sights. The flow of wind had settled, and the bullets would not miss. Every one of the twelve rounds she fired would be absorbed by the boy's back, and his needlelike, slim body should be torn to shreds.

Yes, **that is indeed what should have happened.**

It was in that moment that the rifle in her hands exploded.

The rounds that made contact with the boy had ricocheted. The shells had done a perfect one-eighty, like a videotape rewinding. They had politely jumped back into the barrel of her antitank rifle like a kendama and blasted it to bits.

However, the girl does not possess the physical ability to allow her to ascertain the bullets flying toward her.

These are the only things she knows: first, that some force had destroyed the antitank rifle; second, that uncounted pieces of shrapnel had stabbed into her whole body; and third, that *something* had pierced her right shoulder, which had been pressed against the Metal-eater's stock. It severed her arm like something chomped it off.

In addition, she knows that Accelerator had been hit by her rifle's bullets but still doesn't have a scratch on him.

Finally, she knows that her attempt to snipe him from afar had failed and that Accelerator was now aware of her presence.

That's all she needs to know. In fact, it's more than enough. An intense pain assails her, as if her head were being doused in boiling water, but she pays it no mind. She doesn't have the time. She drags her wrecked body toward the building's emergency stairwell.

Now that her sharpshooting had failed, her one-in-a-million chance to win has vanished. Therefore, she was not fleeing in defeat in order to regroup. Her flight is nothing more than her survival instincts trying to prolong her remaining life by a second or even just a moment.

His footfalls are silent in the twilight. The hunter confidently and soundlessly begins to close in on the girl on the verge of death.

The hunter and the hunted. Their roles were reversed in the blink of an eye, and thus the curtains opened on a murder drama.

CHAPTER 1

Imagine Breaker

Level0(and_More)

1

August 20, 6:10 PM

In the glow of this midsummer evening, Touma Kamijou walked home from his remedial classes, alone and exhausted. *I don't care what the reason is. Going to these summer makeup classes alone isn't good for my mental state during this long summer break,* he thought.

Normally, these "vacation lectures" began on the first day of summer break. His own classes had actually taken place from July 19 through July 28 apparently.

Apparently. That usage of such a vague word was due to the fact that Kamijou was an amnesiac. He had no memories from before July 28. In other words, he didn't really understand why or when the old him had skipped out on those lectures, and he didn't know how he ended up having to pay the bill for it.

Anyway, for some reason…

Kamijou was standing there looking dumbfounded at the juice vending machine sitting in the road by itself.

No. Just wait a second.

Yes—he wanted things to slow down. Touma Kamijou had definitely slid a two thousand yen bill into the machine. So then why on earth wasn't it showing any signs of reacting? All right, he'd admit it.

He was well aware that two thousand yen notes were unusual in this day and age. But it was still *two thousand yen.* The machine hadn't even given a peep after swallowing up such a lump sum. *What's up with this vending machine? Is some mechanical empire rising up in rebellion or what?!* Kamijou yelled at himself, frenetically trying the change return lever over and over.

What rotten luck.

Sadly, if he took out his frustration and started to shake or kick the machine, it would doubtlessly notify the police. He had enough foresight to know that.

The undeveloped areas in the western parts of Tokyo had been cleared away all at once to build Academy City, but despite its rejection of all things occult, everyone who bore witness to Kamijou thought the same unscientific thing: *I guess there really is such a thing as bad luck.* He was just that unfortunate.

As he hung his shoulders in disappointment, he heard the sound of loafers clapping along the ground behind him.

"'Scuse me! Would you quit spacing out in front of that vending machine? If you're not getting anything, then move it, will ya? I'm gonna faint from dehydration if I don't drink something as soon as possible."

No sooner had he heard the voice addressing him from behind than a girl's soft hand grabbed Kamijou's arm and forced him out of the way. Imperfect though he may have been, he was still a boy in his youth. He would have normally expected his heart to start beating a little faster. Right now, though, the only thing on his mind was this unbearable, intimate heat clinging persistently to him.

"What, what?" Kamijou twisted his neck, and there saw a girl who looked like she was in middle school. She had brown shoulder-length hair and a "default" face good enough not to need makeup. She wore a summer sweater over her white short-sleeved blouse. That, along with her gray pleated skirt made him think...*That's the famous Tokiwadai Middle School's uniform, isn't it?* However, he couldn't help but hesitate to call this girl "high-class." She was making the kind of face a salaryman might make after the first time he was disturbed by a packed train, alighting onto the station platform, sick and tired of the whole thing. Maybe the summer heat was getting to her.

...So. I wonder who this is?

Did he know her, or was she a complete stranger just being overly familiar? As an amnesiac, he was worried by this. The most annoying part of having no memories was finding the line between total newcomers and acquaintances. He didn't know how far into this he wanted to go.

Kamijou's gut was saying he knew her. However, he got the feeling that it would be okay if he was to say something mistaken to someone this comfortable around strangers. *Screw it, just say whatever!* he concluded, deciding not to think about it anymore.

"...So. Whaddaya want, you?"

"You know, I have a name! It's Mikoto Misaka! I can't believe you still don't remember it, you total moron!!"

Pale blue sparks flew from her brown bangs with a *snap* as she shouted at him.

Oh, damn, do jokes not work on her?! Without thinking about it, he assumed a defensive posture, and at that moment, a spear of blue-white lightning extended from her forehead like a horn and shot forth at light speed, with him in its sights.

If he had watched it and tried to react, he never would have made it in time. However, his body moved on reflex before the bolt launched. It was almost like it remembered the habit because he'd been on the receiving end of this attack many, many times before.

Kamijou swept his right hand sideways to backhand it, like he was swatting away a passing fly.

Just like that, the javelin of high-tension current in excess of one billion volts split apart like a pillar of water, then disappeared.

Imagine Breaker—the killer of illusions.

It didn't matter if it was a supernatural ability or magic or whatever. It was his unique talent: If something was caused by an "abnormal power," he could touch it with his right hand, and it would cancel it out. That even went for miracles from God himself.

"???"

Kamijou stared at this middle school student (or rather, the unsuccessful homicide criminal). She was giving him a crabby face.

His body had moved unconsciously and evaded the attack. He had experienced this phenomenon once before. That guy, Stiyl Magnus, had whipped out a flame sword, but Kamijou had repelled it without a second thought, purely out of conditioned reflexes left over in his body...

But Kamijou was an amnesiac.

Moreover, even though all his memories were gone, his knowledge still remained. It was quite the odd state of affairs.

At the time, his body had ostensibly reacted by itself. Even though he didn't remember, he had actually been attacked with those flame swords before then.

Which means that this person's someone I'm acquainted with. I see. I know her, do I? Damn it, why the hell did I only know people like this?!

"Would you stop looking at me like you're about to cry?" Mikoto placed her hands on her hips. "Anyway, if you don't have anything else to do, then move it. I've *totally* got something to do with this vending machine."

"Uh..."

His eyes bounced between the vending machine and the girl who named herself as Mikoto Misaka.

She didn't have a shred of consideration for the situation, and she was also the culprit of an attempted murder...but would it be okay *not* to tell her about how he knew this vending machine would definitely eat her money just because of that? Well, it wasn't quite that he wanted to not see her disappointed; he was more scared of a homicidal rage when she came to attack him afterward, which she would inevitably do.

"That vending machine. Seems like it just eats your money."

"I know that," answered Mikoto succinctly. Okay, now *he* was the one who didn't understand *her* intentions.

"??? You're gonna put money in it even though you know it'll eat it? Is this the donation box for some kinda shrine?"

"You're an utter moron. I have a trick, all right? A trick to make the juice come out without actually putting any money in."

"…"

He got a bad feeling about this. He got a *really* bad feeling about this. This trick…He figured that she must use it a whole ton on a daily basis if she was calling it a "trick." To repeat, Kamijou's two thousand yen note had been eaten by the machine. Could the reason it was malfunctioning like this possibly be…

"Tokiwadai Middle School style—Old Lady Forty-Five-Degree-Angle Machine-Restarting Strike!"

Remarkably, along with the ridiculous ending shout of "*Chaysaa!*," Mikoto delivered a high kick to the side of the vending machine, while wearing a skirt.

There was a deafening *thump!* Then they heard something inside the machine rattling around and falling, and shortly after, cans of juice appeared in the dispenser.

"It's all worn-out, so the springs holding in the juice are loose, you know? Trouble is, you never know what's gonna come out…Uh, what's up with you?"

"Absolutely nothing," Kamijou replied in perfect monotone.

Under her skirt were gym short pants. Somehow, he felt like his dreams had been ruined.

"Wait, so if it's *passed down* at Tokiwadai, does that mean *all* the rich girls there do that?"

"That's what all-female schools are all about. Don't go having weird dreams about girls, got it?"

"…" Kamijou thought it was a pretty harsh reality. "That wasn't it. I wanted to ask: Isn't the reason the vending machine is broken in the first place because you all come along every single day and gang up on the thing?!"

"It's no problem! What are you so mad about? It's not like it's hurting you, right?"

"…"

"Hmm? By the way, how did ya figure out this machine was a money eater…" She quieted for a moment before finishing. "…Did your money get eaten?"

"…"

"Huh? It did? It really did?! Hey, quit making fists and trembling like that. Give me a straight answer! Were you spacing out because the vending machine ate your money?!"

"...What would you do if you heard the answer?"

"That's simple, I'd take a picture with my cell phone and send the idiot's face out to the world— I'm joking, I'm joking! Stop shuffling forward like you're gauging distance, it's scary!"

Kamijou exhaled and let the strength flow out of him.

Taking it out on her wouldn't bring his two thousand yen back. That two thousand yen had originally been placed in his wallet with the intention of buying some fireworks or something for the free-loading sister in white awaiting his return at the dorms. There was no point in pondering that now, though. *Losers should just act like losers and follow their homing instincts or something.* Kamijou let his shoulders fall and turned his back to Mikoto.

She looked at that easily readable back of his and, with her hands still on her waist, breathed a pretty exasperated sigh.

"Wait a second, you. So how much got eaten exactly?"

"...I'm not telling. I can't. I don't want to."

He looked at this girl. They'd just met, but he didn't think straight up telling *her* he'd lost two thousand yen would lead to her saying, "Oh, you poor thing!" Her responding with a "ga-ha-ha-wa-ha-ha!" laugh, like a warring states–era general, would probably make more sense.

Then her face grew slightly more serious (perhaps, somehow, feeling *something* like responsibility).

"I won't laugh. I promise. And by the way, I'll even get back the money it ate."

What could these friendly skills be?! Kamijou wondered, his eyes sparkling. His thoughts never arrived at the realization that this was all Mikoto's fault in the first place for kicking the vending machine all the time.

So there Kamijou was, a little scared of being labeled an idiot who managed to get two thousand yen stuck in a machine. However, when Mikoto said, "I said, I won't laugh! I really won't, okay? I really, definitely won't laugh!" he decided to confess, defeated.

"…Two thousand yen."

"Two thousand? Why are you making a fuss about such pocket change?" After saying this, she stopped short as it dawned on her. "Wait, two thousand yen? Wait, you mean like, a two thousand yen note?! Wow, I wanna see! I totally want to see that! I thought all those bills were extinct! He-he…Aha-ha-ha-ha! Of course the vending machine would bug out. Two thousand yen notes aren't even in convenience store registers these days! Aha-ha-ha-ha, eek!"

Mikoto was getting excited at something weird. Kamijou looked at her, shouted, "You liar!" and automatically buried his face in his hands. *That's* why he didn't want to tell her it was a two thousand yen note. Him using it on a vending machine also strongly implied he was trying to exchange it for lower currency amounts. This was a two thousand yen note they were talking about here. Even a department store clerk with a perfectly sculpted, smiling expression would definitely let out a grunt and falter, even if only for a moment.

"I see. Well then, you better start praying that two thousand yen bill comes out…I won't accept it if you give me two one thousand yen bills, got it, you piece of junk?"

Mikoto stood herself in front of the vending machine, then slowly thrust the palm of her right hand toward the coin insert slot.

Suddenly Kamijou wasn't so sure about all of this.

"But how are you gonna get the money out of there?"

"How?"

She gave him a look of blank amazement.

"Like this."

A moment later, bluish-white sparks launched out of the palm of Mikoto's hand and struck the vending machine.

A roaring *whump!* thundered, and the extremely heavy-looking machine wobbled back and forth like it had been rammed by a sumo wrestler. A mountain of black smoke erupted from the gaps between its metal fittings as if this were some kind of gag manga.

Kamijou paled. In fact, his face turned pure white.

"Huh? That's weird. I didn't plan on blasting it that hard. Ah, looks like a ton of juice is coming out. Hey, your two thousand yen note didn't come out, but there's, uh, definitely at least two thousand yen's worth of juice cans coming out. Is that okay?…Hey, why are you running away so desperately?! Heeeey!"

He didn't turn back. He sprinted at full speed in an effort to put every centimeter, every millimeter he could between him and that vending machine.

He knew because he experienced all sorts of bad luck at every turn. He could see the future one second from now clearly.

D-damn it! I don't know why, but I get the distinct feeling this has happened before!!

As soon as he thought that…

Though the alarms on the vending machine would remain silent even if kicked, they started to blare with all their might, so that everything could hear, as if it was mercilessly spewing out all of its pent-up frustration.

2

He didn't really remember where or how he ran.

What he could say for sure was that he had sprinted all out for about ten minutes.

The next thing he realized, he was seated on the bench at a bus stop in the shopping district. Exhausted, he was staring up at the August sky, which was dyed in orange by the light of the sunset. A blimp was floating through the air. On its side was a large screen, lazily spilling out Academy City's news for the day, regarding the announcement that a Mizuho Agency, an organization researching muscular dystrophy, had withdrawn from business.

"Quit blissfully running away from reality and hold your drinks, will ya? This is your share in the first place."

Sitting next to him was Mikoto, sighing in exasperation and throwing a whole bunch of juice cans at him. For her part, she was gazing calmly at the propellers on a wind generator, spinning round and round. She might have been a little down in the dumps at having failed to control her power.

"...Kamijou was afraid that somehow, the moment he takes this juice, he'll evolve from bystander to accomplice. Wait, don't throw it at me like I'm a garbage can—hey, that's hot! Why the hell is hot red bean soup in there?!"

"The point was to get it to malfunction, so I can't choose what kind I get!"

"But I'm getting some pretty clear evil signals with this black soybean cider and this condensed kinako milk!"

"Hmm? Hey, count your blessings. You should be thanking Miss Mikoto's good fortune for not pulling the two demons—the guarana vegetable juice and the strawberry oden soup!"

Academy City was, put another way, a city of experiments.

Its countless universities and research institutions enjoyed testing their "products" in practical applications, so prototypes like garbage-collecting automatons and self-driving police robots filled every corner of the city. And well, this meant that the product lineups on convenience store shelves and in vending machines differed from normal cities, too...

"...It's all different, but I've got half a mind to put in an inquiry regarding the fact that it's still the same money we students are paying."

"Come on, it's fine! It's okay to be filled with dreams and ambitions and advance one step at a time, isn't it? Oh, if you're not gonna drink that coconut cider, then I'll take it." Mikoto took one of the macabre juice cans from Kamijou's arms. "Anyway, you run away from things too easily—including from this one can of juice. It's like...How do I put it?...You're actually strong, but you make people *think* you're just a weak idiot? Whenever Miss Mikoto sees that, she gets half a mind to say a thing or two about it."

"...I wonder why it's only the people who say stuff that totally misses the mark who seem so weirdly egotistical?"

"What was that?" Mikoto looked at Kamijou with the face of a belligerent drunk. "...I don't think it's all that far off, really. There are lots of weaklings who go through life trembling in fear, and strong people live haughtily. I think that's only natural. But you're different, right? You have the kind of power that can easily force one of the seven Level Fives in Academy City to back down, so why on earth do you flee all over the town whenever you're chased by so much as a hoodlum or a Chihuahua that got off its leash?"

"???"

Mikoto's words were chock-full of confidence, but Kamijou couldn't remember any of it.

If that *was* the case, then either Mikoto's words were a bad guess, or else...Could she know **about his unknown past?** Unable to figure out which it was, Kamijou decided to vaguely bring himself in line with the conversation.

"You know, you should brag more that you defeated Mikoto Misaka, the Railgun. Not doing so is an **inexcusable offense to the defeated party**. I mean, don't you see? From now on, everyone will think this their whole lives about me: '*Mikoto Misaka* lost to a man who gets chased around by hoodlums and Chihuahuas off their collars?'" Mikoto took a swig of the coconut cider. "You won against me. So at the very least, you should take responsibility as the victor, or else you'll cause me trouble. I am one of *only seven* Level Fives in Academy City! At least try hard enough so that I can stick out my chest and say that I lost to a person like you, fairly and openly."

"What are you talking about? I've got no interest in Edo period Bushido morals, so..."

Before he could finish, Kamijou noticed an odd, out-of-place feeling in that last thing she said.

You won against me?

Which means...Did I, the humble Touma Kamijou, take a high-class girl from a high-class school like Tokiwadai Middle School, push her down, get on top of her, ball my fists, and beat the hell out of her until she cried that she was sorry and would never do it again, is that it? I see, it's only natural that such a man's brain cells would have broken and his memories gotten destroyed, and also, what the hell were you doing while I didn't remember, and also, a girl telling me to "take responsibility" sounds an awful lot like a threat, you know!!

"Uh, urrrrrrrrrrrrrrrrrr...!!"

"? Hey, wait, why are you getting all groany like that?" Mikoto sighed. "Man, you're really a pain in the ass, you know that? What, did you pull that from some *shounen* manga or something?" She folded her arms and exhaled like she took offense to it.

Kamijou, grasping his head in dismay, didn't notice.

"It's that way you do things, you know? Where you never throw your own punches. You just let your opponents beat you to a pulp and perfectly guard all of it. It's so conceited and annoying, and yet it's definitely effective. I won't allow it!"

"...Uurrrrrrr...uh?"

He refocused on what Mikoto was going on about, still moaning with his head in his hands.

I never throw my own punches? So then, this was the same kind of power relation as a parent smiling and calming down a child? One who took a joke too seriously and was shaking his fists in the air or something?

I never raised a hand against girls, even if I was fighting a lightning user?

...

...That's not bad, Touma Kamijou.

"Huh. I really can't stand you when you look confident, you know that?" Mikoto sounded disinterested. "Here, whatever, just drink your juice. Man, getting a gift like this directly from Miss Mikoto... If you were one of my underclassmen, you'd be swooning and fainting right now!"

"Fainting? There isn't a soul alive who'd be happy about these cans of juice that just barely fulfill the food hygiene laws. Besides, this isn't some *shoujo* manga, so there're no *love stories* in an all girls' school."

"...Well. It would be sweet if it *was* just at *shoujo* manga levels." For some reason, Mikoto averted her eyes. "Everything's pretty busy, okay? Or maybe I should say muddy. You want me to tell you what I get called at school? It'll blow you away!·

"We-he-haa-hah…" Mikoto laughed, without any strength behind it. But then…

"Big Sister?"

Suddenly, the bell-like voice of a girl sounded out near them, and Mikoto made a face like ice had been plunged into her back. The corners of her mouth twitched, and she scowled deeply.

Bi…?! Big…!!

Kamijou caught his breath at the unexpected shock. *What is this?!* He quickly jerked his head to look behind him and saw a girl who looked to be in her first year of middle school, wearing the same uniform as Mikoto, standing a little away from them. With brown hair in pigtails, she clasped her hands in front of her and made her eyes sparkle.

"Oh my, Big Sister! My, oh my! I thought those silly remedial classes didn't suit you, but I never would have guessed you'd be using them as an excuse for *this*!"

Kamijou looked beside him; Mikoto looked about ready to panic. It's not like he had any power, but he strangely felt like she had transmitted an internal cry straight to his mind, forbidding him from butting in.

She pressed on her temples like she had a headache and began to speak to the mystery girl.

"Umm…I just want to be sure. What might you be referring to when you say *this*?"

"Well, obviously, it was in order to rendezvous with this gentleman here, was it not?"

Sparks came from Mikoto's hair with a *crackle*.

The girl in pigtails didn't mind, though. This time, she flashed a full smile at Kamijou, who was currently watching blankly, and approached their bench terrifyingly quickly. *Oh, shit, she came over here!* He was about to jolt off the bench in spite of himself, but before he could, the girl grabbed hold of his hand and covered it with both of hers.

"Pleased to make your acquaintance, gentleman. My name is Kuroko Shirai, and I'm Big Sister's *outrider*."

"Uh-huh." Kamijou struggled to find a reaction. His gaze was steadily lowering to the hand she had clasped.

"By the way, if this is all it takes to get you flustered, she might have to worry about you being prone to…adultery, you know?"

Kamijou sputtered like he was a volcano about to erupt. Mikoto wobbled up out of her seat beside him and said, "Listen here, you… Does this weirdo *look* like my boyfriend?!"

As she delivered those subtly wounding words, Mikoto let loose a spear of lightning from her bangs.

But just before the pale blue electricity hit her, Kuroko Shirai let go of Kamijou's hand. The next time he blinked, she had disappeared into thin air without a word.

Mikoto clicked her teeth. "She used that stupid teleport of hers. I swear to God if you start spreading strange rumors, I'm coming after you, damn it!"

She fired a few more bolts at the empty space. People passing by gathered their attention to the Level Five *buzz-buzz. Oh, jeez, how do I get her to calm down now?!* wondered Kamijou with his head in his hands, when all of a sudden, a voice came at them from behind the bench.

"Big Sister?"

Not again?! Kamijou turned around.

Behind the bench stood another Mikoto Misaka.

"Eh?"

There was no doubt that the person standing there was Mikoto Misaka. She had brown shoulder-length hair, a well-featured face, a white short-sleeved blouse, a summer sweater, and a pleated skirt. There she was—a perfect Mikoto Misaka, from her height to her clothes and smaller articles.

However…

Kamijou returned his eyes to the bench seat next to him. Brown shoulder-length hair, a well-featured face, a white short-sleeved blouse, a summer sweater, and a pleated skirt—Mikoto Misaka was obviously sitting right there.

The difference was that the girl standing behind the bench was wearing something akin to night-vision goggles on her forehead as if they were swimming goggles. In addition, the glint in her eyes made it seem like they weren't focused on any one thing, but rather were trying to chase everything coming into her sight. Those ambiguously unfocused eyes intently followed the back of Mikoto's head.

"...Wait, what? There's more of you?! Misaka Unit Two!"

Kamijou was flabbergasted. He looked at the faces of the two Mikoto Misakas in turn. The one on the bench next to him had a similarly astonished look, but the one standing behind the bench was staring at them without a trace of an expression.

"So," he hazarded, looking over his shoulder, "who might you be?"

The girl behind the bench shifted her eyes to him without moving her neck.

"I am her little sister, Misaka replies, quickly and precisely."

"..."

What an odd way of talking, he mused, though he decided not to say it. There were too many people close to Kamijou who talked funny. He didn't realize that he was one of them himself, though.

"But your name is 'something Misaka,' and your first name is Misaka? You're not Misaka Misaka, you know. You normally put your given name there, right? Wouldn't it get confusing if you went by Misaka at your house?"

"Well, Misaka's name is Misaka, Misaka replies immediately."

"..."

She can't actually *be named Misaka Misaka, but it seems there's some weird, unspoken rules coming into play here.*

Kamijou looked to Mikoto to throw him a life preserver, but he clammed up again when he saw her face. For some reason, she was silently glaring at her (apparently identical) younger sister.

"I-I see, you're her little sister. Wow, you two look a lot alike. Could it be that your heights and weights are the same, too?"

Mikoto had been staring at her little sister for a while.

"We're identical on the genetic level, Misaka replies. Also, how rude he is to bring up the topic of body weight with a girl, she says to herself."

Mikoto had been staring at her little sister for quite a while now.

"…" *What a strange person*, thought Kamijou. "If you're the same on a genetic level, then that means you're twins! Hmm. I've never seen identical twins before, but man, they really do look alike, huh? Anyway, what do you need, Miss Twin? Going home with your big sister?"

Mikoto had been staring at her little sister for a long, long while at this point.

"What a fresh mouth this flippant jerk has, Misaka thinks, but she swallows her true opinion and answers his question. Misaka detected an equivalent power in a zone six hundred meters in radius centered on Misaka, so I came to take a look…"

It seemed perfectly logical that similar abilities would appear for identical twins.

It was logical, but…Kamijou finally started to get scared of the look on Mikoto's face.

That's bad…Is she the kind of person who hates showing her family's faces and stuff to her friends on parents' day at school? he pondered.

"…There was a broken vending machine at the site, and you two are in possession of a large amount of juice. I never thought my sister would have a hand in petty theft, says Misaka, clucking her tongue." Little Misaka was still standing straight and stiff. "What means have you used to win my sister over? inquires Misaka, just to be sure."

She was placing him under strange suspicions, so there was no other choice but to continue the conversation.

"Hey, the principal offender here was *her*. I was just a bystander!"

"Making false claims constitutes a crime, answers Misaka. As a result of measuring the front of the vending machine via its reflectivity, I discovered that the most recent fingerprints left on it were yours, accuses Misaka with veritable proof."

"You must be kidding! Lightning users can even figure *that* out?!"

"I am kidding, Misaka replies straightly."

"..."

"..."

HELP ME, thought Kamijou, tugging on Mikoto's shoulder but still looking at Little Misaka.

But no matter how long he waited, she didn't say anything to her. *That's weird*, he thought. *I've only known her for ten minutes, but I can clearly tell that she'd just keep talking by herself even if no one asked her to. How is it possible that she's keeping silent now that someone is saying bad stuff about her?*

"...?"

Kamijou casually looked toward the girl in the seat next to him. Then...

"...You! Why the hell are you just loafing around in a place like this?!"

Suddenly, an angry yell exploded from Mikoto, who had been quiet until now.

Whoa! Kamijou nearly leaned back from the ear-splitting shout that cut them off. That shrill voice girls have pierced into his earholes and a sensation not unlike brain freeze assaulted him.

After the one mad outburst, she shut up again.

As if she was waiting for Little Misaka to reply.

They were enveloped by an empty silence, like the kind that happens after lightning strikes.

A blimp was wandering through the night sky. The big screen plastered on its side was repeating today's news that a new computer virus called HDC.Cerberus was wreaking havoc on the Internet. The voice announcing it resounded cryptically.

Below all that, Little Misaka, still standing rigid as a pole, looked into Mikoto's eyes with a dazed stare.

"If you must ask, I am in training right now, Misaka responds concisely."

"Tra..."

Mikoto sucked in her breath like someone had hit her in the back, then turned her eyes away. She muttered something under her breath, but Kamijou didn't catch it.

"??? In training? Did your sister enter Judgment or something?"

When someone with the rank of student hears the word *training*, Judgment is usually the thing that immediately comes to mind.

As one might have figured out from Mikoto's power, abilities boast more capacity for casualties than a poorly handled knife. With more than 2.3 million espers in Academy City, there would, of course, be a specialized agency for dealing with the ones who go out of control.

There are two offices that suppress rampaging espers: the Anti-Skills, a force of teachers wielding next-generation weaponry, and Judgment, made up of espers elected from each of the schools.

Both the Anti-Skills and the members of Judgment are nothing more than run-of-the-mill teachers and students when one got right down to it. Because of that, however, they must sign nine contractual agreements, take thirteen different aptitude tests, and overcome four months of training before they're able to call themselves *professionals*.

Mikoto clapped her hands together in front of her face and, for some reason, excellently averted her eyes from his. "Um. Ah, Judgment? Ah, yeah, that's it. That's what's going on, so when things like this happen, I get in a bunch of trouble. A bunch. Or maybe a crunch?"

She said all this in a fantastically fishy tone of voice.

"Hey, why does all this suddenly sound like a phone scam? The more you talk, the less information you're giving me."

"N-no, it isn't! I'm speaking distinctly and clearly, yeah, distincti-clearly!" Then Mikoto turned her eyes to her sister. "It's just that there's a lot I need to say. A lot. Hey, Sis, would you come over here a sec?"

"Huh? No, Misaka has her own schedule to keep, says—"

"Forget that." Mikoto stared her younger sister in the eyes. **"Come over here."**

Her oddly level voice weighed on Kamijou's mind for some reason.

It's not like Mikoto really *did* anything. She just looked at the face of her sister, smiled, and said one thing. But that one thing...An unknown whirlpool of emotion within it stuck right in his core.

Mikoto looked at him. The only thing there now was the face of a completely normal, if loud, middle school student.

"Well, we're heading down this way. You should be mindful of your curfew, too!"

She left behind Kamijou, still sitting on the bench, and wrapped an arm around her sister's shoulders. The absolutely identical pair of girls started walking down the wide road.

He slumped in his seat. Then, gazing at the blimp floating along in the night sky, he murmured, "Seems like a complicated"—he paused—"family situation, I guess?"

3

If he needed a problem, he had them in spades.

"Yeah, that's right! What the heck am I gonna do with all this juice?"

Kamijou stared befuddled at the mountain of nineteen drink cans on the bench (Mikoto had consumed just one: the coconut cider), but in the end, he was going to have to physically carry them all. *Three hundred and fifty times nineteen, so 6.65 kilograms, huh, I guess it's what they say: the dust piling up and stuff.* His futile calculations brought him even deeper into despair. He was in about the same mental state as an acrophobic who had just carelessly peeked beneath a suspension bridge.

And with this and that, Kamijou tottered back home in the red afternoon light with an armful of cans. The road leading through the residential district was narrow, with nothing but student dorms on either side, and there weren't many cars. But it was the one kind of place where if you started thinking that a car *wouldn't* come along, you might be sent flying by the rear end of a car that suddenly leaped out of a garage in reverse.

Unfortunate though he was, even Kamijou wasn't accustomed

enough to bad luck to smile and be killed by a car five minutes away from home.

Getting back's gonna be a hike, thought Kamijou, psyching himself up and readjusting the juice he was carrying.

The cold cans had been in his hands like this for a while, and they were starting to steal away quite a bit of his body heat. *Why do I have to be nearly frozen to death during this stupidly hot Japanese summer?!* he lamented to himself.

All of a sudden, Kamijou noticed a tennis ball on the ground at his feet, and he snapped out of his thoughts. *Was someone playing with it and just left it here afterward?* he wondered.

"Whoa, there."

He had been just barely about to step on it, but he stopped his upraised foot and shifted it a little to the side to try and avert disaster. *Jeez, that was close. If I had tripped over this thing, it would have sucked!* he thought…

…when suddenly, the wind blew.

The swaying ball slid into the space between his foot and the ground as if the whole thing had been calculated.

"Egh! Wait, you little—!"

He had already started to put his body weight into that leg—he couldn't stop his foot at this point. All his weight came down on the ball perfectly, and he toppled over backward.

There was so much juice in his hands that he couldn't fall safely, either. His back slammed into the ground, driving all the air out of his lungs, and he writhed in place without even enough to muster a "what rotten luck."

The cans of juice that he *was* carrying scattered and rolled all over the place, clinking and clanking, but for the moment, he just laid there sprawled out and took some deep breaths. He even figured, *Well, they're just cans of juice, so it probably doesn't matter if some of them get dented.*

"D-damn it. What did I do to deserve this…," he huffed, finally sitting himself upright. Seeing the nineteen cans spread out over such a large area made him feel hopeless. "Do I really hafta pick up six kilos of this stuff again?" he whined to himself. Still, it wasn't like he had any other solutions. When all was said and done, he was going to have to gather them up by himself, all alone.

As he bent over to do so, a shadow fell directly over him.

...A cloud?

What's this? He automatically looked up.

Mikoto Misaka was standing there.

Whoa?!

Kamijou flinched, then took a step back from the crushing pressure of the silent middle school girl looking down at him.

"You, uh...Huh? Didn't you go somewhere with your little sister? I mean, if you want more juice, I can give you two or three cans."

"..." Mikoto didn't respond to what he said.

That's odd, he thought, before remembering something. Mikoto had told him this, with a bit of lightning thrown in, just before: that he should take the minimum responsibility as the victor, since he defeated her. That he should act in a way that she can stick out her chest and declare, fairly and openly, that she had lost to this man.

How was he supposed to do that right now? The Touma Kamijou in question had just stepped on a tennis ball, fallen onto the pavement, flung cans of juice all over the road, and was in the process of bending over and picking up the cans, feeling sorry for himself. And finally...

Gah?! She got too close, this is bad, at this angle I can see up her skirt— Hey, wait, wasn't she just wearing gym short pants before, why did she class-change into panties?!

Despite currently being confused about a few different things, he was aware looking straight at it would make anyone mad.

Mikoto looked down at Kamijou with eyes that seemed to have lost all emotion.

"If you require assistance, I will help you, suggests Misaka with a sigh."

"???"

Kamijou stared for a moment in suspicion at Mikoto. She was far from sighing—she was breathing so quietly it struck him as strange, but...

And that was when he finally noticed the night-vision goggles in her hands.

"Oh, okay, it's the sister. You know, you really do look like Mikoto."

"...Mikoto...? Misaka responds. Oh, you mean my big sister."

"Who else would I be talking about?" *She's going at her own pace as always,* he noted. "...I see. You're her little sister. No wonder I thought she class-changed away from short pants."

"Short...?"

"No, that was just me talking to myself! Uh, anyway, right! What are those rough-looking army goggles you've got there?"

"Unlike my big sister, Misaka has no skill at seeing the flow of electricity or magnetism, so Misaka requires an apparatus to visualize them, Misaka politely explains in detail."

"..."

Don't go thinking that you sound polite just because you used some fancy words, Kamijou said to himself.

"The heat and humidity were high, so I removed them. However, if you feel it is necessary, then I will equip them, suggests Misaka."

Little Misaka pulled the goggles over her forehead, muttering something to herself.

"Hm. Huh? But didn't you go with your sis before?"

"Misaka came from that direction, says Misaka, pointing."

Little Misaka pointed down the road. For some reason it was the completely wrong direction.

"?" Kamijou canted his head, confused.

"In any case, what will you do about the littered juice cans? asks Misaka. If you leave them here, it will conflict with the road traffic law and you may be fined any amount up to 150,000 yen, she adds."

"...Right, sorry. I'll pick them all up, so go away."

He knew that she hadn't said that in a nasty or bitter way or anything, but being told to get something done *now* because he was bothering people around him managed to touch a nerve.

As he silently picked up the cans of juice one by one…

"If necessary, Misaka will help as well, Misaka proposes."

"Eh? It's okay, I'll do it. Besides, you've got no reason to help me, do you?"

But then, at the worst possible moment, a small truck came rolling down the residential roadway. It screeched to a halt in front of Kamijou and Misaka, and its driver honked the horn at them a few times in exasperation.

"…"

Without another word, Little Misaka began to collect the juice making a mess on the road. He felt a little ashamed at making a girl he didn't really know help him fix his own blunder. However, the truck's horn had been beeping at them to hurry up since it arrived, so he couldn't even say that. Having no other choice, he settled on the gender equality option: each of them picking up half.

He found himself unable to leave it like that, though, so he said shortly, "Sorry. I'll buy you an ice cream at the convenience store later or something, so I hope you……!"

As he was saying that, he looked at Little Misaka again and caught his breath in spite of himself.

The defenselessly crouching Little Misaka wasn't giving a thought to her particularly short skirt. He got a peek at some kind of white-and-blue stripes between her legs.

Still squatting, Little Misaka looked up at him, her face blank.

"…What is it? Misaka queries."

"Ee…! N-nothing, it's nothing, okay? It's absolutely nothing, okay?"

"You say that, but I am detecting dilated pupils, ragged breathing, and abnormalities in pulse are being detected, evaluates Misaka objectively. In conclusion, you are in a state of excitement, are you not? says Misa—"

"No, nothing! It's really nothing! I'm really sorry!"

"?"

Misaka's head tilted, puzzled, like she wanted to ask who he was apologizing to.

Then the truck blared that miserable horn again. Kamijou got a move on like someone had kicked him in the butt and went back to picking up the juice.

Once they were finished, the truck violently proceeded on its way, indeed seeming quite angry. Incidentally, as the truck drove by, Little Misaka's skirt flipped up. She still didn't push it back down.

Hmm…I think I might have figured out how to tell these sisters apart, sighed Kamijou. Mikoto didn't leave herself this unprotected—she wore gym short pants under her skirt.

"Now then, where shall I bring this juice? asks Misaka, her arms full of juice cans."

"Eh? No, I can do that myself, all right?"

"Now then, where shall I bring this juice? insists Misaka."

"I said it's okay, you don't have to. It's not your responsibility or anything."

"Just tell me already."

He thought he felt her voice growing sharp. He gave up and decided to let Little Misaka carry it.

Fortunately, his dormitory was only a five-minute walk away. It was a dreary place, what with all the identical buildings lined up next to each other. Actually, it was apparently the number one wind turbine location in Academy City or something, since the building winds all funneled into the same direction.

They slipped into what was practically a back alley, then he turned the entrance doorknob, casting doubt as to whether or not the security systems were actually working, and they headed for the elevator.

As they headed there, a cleaning robot appeared in front of them and approached. It was basically an oil drum, eight centimeters tall and forty in diameter, with tires and a revolving mop plugged onto it.

The description thus far wouldn't have been an unusual sight in Academy City, but the next part was a bit different. Atop the flat head of the cleaning drone, there was a thirteen- or fourteen-year-old maid, meekly sitting seiza, kneeling with legs tucked underneath her thighs.

"Heya, Touma Kamijou!"

Maika Tsuchimikado. She was the stepsister of Kamijou's neighbor, Motoharu Tsuchimikado. She apparently wore a maid uniform because she was going to housekeeping school (read: a maid school). At first she might have looked like a runaway who had fled the girls' dorms after something bad happened so she could take a breather. However, it hadn't been very long at all since he lost his memories. He kept on seeing her around here, so it seemed like she was just routinely sneaking into the place.

"My air conditioner was broken today so I came to sleep over! I think my big brother and I are both gonna get pretty loud tonight, so please have some patience, okay?"

"...Huh, housekeeping school must be a pain, huh. You've got no summer break!"

"Well. Our school teaches that true maids don't need any off time, you know! There's no Saturday or Sunday for maids in training, so if they don't enact a couple of days off during the week here and there, we'd all up and collapse."

"But is a *slacker maid* really in demand in this glacial epoch?"

"Actually, in a way, 'incomplete' maids are in higher demand than the perfect ones, but...Oh. By the way, Touma Kamijou. Are those the spoils of war from Operation Win the Lottery?"

"No, I paid for these properly (probably). I got 'em from a bit of a dirty job, but you can have one if you want."

"If you have green tea, then I'll take that."

"...Sure, if you count green tea *milk* as green tea."

Maika Tsuchimikado ended up reaching out with her tiny hand and taking the powdered green tea milk out of Kamijou's arms. Then the cleaning robot diverted its path around Kamijou and Little Misaka. Maika, still sitting seiza, waved her arm good-bye in a long arc.

"One last thing. The first trick to giving shelter to runaway girls! Don't leave them alone in your room since noon. In a city in peacetime, the easiest way to feed them is to let them loose outside and then pick them up when night falls. If you leave one in your room

24-7, 365 days a year, the noise from her living there will leak in no time and the neighboring residents might catch on. And also, that nun is making a really big ruckus in your room, did you know?"

The cleaning drone carrying the sitting girl rolled away somewhere.

"You have hobbies of imprisoning girls? attempts Misaka, a little seriously."

"Don't get all serious. I'm just harboring a freeloader," Kamijou declared, though…What *did* the law have to say on the matter? He earnestly hoped this wouldn't be termed "abducting a minor," or anything along those lines.

Kamijou and Little Misaka boarded the elevator, the cables of which seemed like they would snap if a sumo wrestler got in, and headed for the seventh floor.

Ding-dong came a cheap-sounding electric noise, heralding the elevator's arrival on the seventh story. His dormitory building was roughly rectangular, so the only thing greeting them as they stepped off was a straight hallway.

At the other end—and *only* in front of the door to his room—the metal railing had oddly been replaced. Kamijou had gathered it had happened before losing his memory, so he didn't know why, but it *appeared* that some idiot had blown off the railing with fire. When he looked closely, there were spots here and there on the walls and floor that looked like new as well.

Crouched before the door were Index and Aisa Himegami, facing each other and looking at the calico. They had their hands extended to it and were fawning over it. The cat, surrounded and being pampered by two sets of hands, was rolling around the floor.

"…Huh, what are they doing over there? Hey! What's wrong, you lose the key to the room and lock yourselves out?" he called. The two of them looked over.

"Ah, it's Touma! No, Sphinx has fleas, so we were— Hey, wait! Touma, you brought along another girl again!"

The girl who cried out was Index, a fourteen- or fifteen-year-old girl. Though her name was 100 percent fake, she was clad in a plush, gold-embroidered nun's habit with a white background; it looked like a teacup. Apparently in some world she was called "the Index of Forbidden Books," but Kamijou had been giving her the decidedly more *subtle* treatment of "freeloader who appeared without my knowing."

"Perhaps you were born under *those* stars. You start to build up the various routes. As if you were triggering flags."

The girl who lazily remarked on him was Aisa Himegami, a sixteen- or seventeen-year-old girl. She looked the gold standard of a shrine maiden, with long black hair and a red-and-white priestess uniform. Despite that, a large silver cross hanging from her neck stood out against them. As well it should—it was apparently a barrier made to seal the power she held called "Deep Blood."

Then he remembered that Index had told him something along these lines about it:

"Touma, Touma. Don't touch Aisa's Celtic cross, okay? After all, it's a cross extracted from just the part of the Walking Church that maintains a minimal barrier. Hmm, if we compared it to a normal church, I guess it would be like carrying around just the big cross on its roof?"

"Huh. So that means if I touch it with my right hand, it'll break."

"...Yeah, just like the time with my habit."

"Hm? What? I couldn't hear you."

"Nothing! I didn't say anything, and I'm not thinking anything!"

After that, Index's face flushed for some reason, and she had bitten into his head as if she was taking something out on him. Anyway, the gist of it seemed to be that he should never, ever touch that cross.

Incidentally, now that the cross had sealed her powers, Himegami had been judged "talentless" by the elite private school she was attending and was about to get kicked out. It wasn't unusual for private schools to have an enrollment criteria of being a Level Two Adept or above. If you consider how athletes who got into a college on sports scholarships are treated when they injure themselves and are unable to exercise, it should be easy to understand her situation.

In reality, if she just took off the cross, Deep Blood would apparently reactivate, but she didn't seem to have any plans to take it off ever again.

With this and that, she had automatically been driven from her student dormitory. If she left Academy City, though, she might be targeted by sorcerers seeking the power of Deep Blood. From what he heard, she was wandering around aimlessly wondering what she should do when who should arrive but Kamijou's homeroom teacher, Miss Komoe. She picked her up and turned Himegami into a freeloader or something.

Some might think it extremely unlikely to just run into someone like that in a city as big as this one, but spots where runaway girls naturally gather in actually exist. Miss Komoe was a specialist in things like social psychology, environmental psychology, behavioral psychology, and traffic psychology. He heard that she made a hobby of going around to those kinds of places, finding delinquent girls, and bringing them under her guardianship. Kamijou, meanwhile, got this weird ill omen that once summer break ended, he'd be in for a "shocking" transfer student event, effectively utilizing the kind of flags *she* had raised.

Himegami glanced at the mountain of juice cans he was carrying and asked, "Anyway. What is that mountain of treasure? Are you a sickly child? Who can't drink tap water?"

"'Course not. Besides, juice is worse for your body anyway." He sighed at her. "Come on, Index, you're on sweet stuff duty, aren't you?"

"Mgh. I like juice, but I *don't* like those 'pull tab' things. Touma, open it for me!"

Unaccustomed to modern culture, Index apparently wasn't able to open the pull tabs on the cans. It wasn't that she didn't know how or that she wasn't strong enough to—it was more like she thought, *Uh, if I try to open this too hard, I'll break a nail.*

The pull tab–phobic Index turned her gaze to Little Misaka, who was standing next to Kamijou, also with an armful of juice.

"Sigh. Man, Touma, your encounter rate with problem girls is too high! And besides, you wouldn't listen if one told you not to get involved anyway. So who is this girl, where's she from, and what's she do?"

"If you want my personal view. I think she is an ill-fated girl on the run from a mysterious organization."

"Would you be quiet? You're one-sidedly treating every single person around me like they're unlucky," Kamijou complained, juice cans in hand. "...Anyway, you said something before I can't let go, didn't you? What do you mean by the cat has fleas?"

"Yeah," Index replied, nodding in assent. "One morning I woke up and Sphinx was covered in fleas. I think your futon is probably a total mess and stuff."

"Don't 'and stuff' me! Don't put things like cats into futons! In addition, all the hair it sheds is gonna be a pain in the ass! Wait, I had been thinking I was itchy for some reason. Was that what happened?! Agh!" Kamijou cried. "And also, why are you leaving the room alone?! Won't it turn into some demon cave with all the reproduced fleas?! So that's why you two are outside! Damn it!"

The doorknob was right in front of him, but he hesitated to open it.

Then, disregarding him, Index plunged a hand into her sleeve and started rustling around for something.

"...Uh, Index. So why are you taking green leaves out of your clothes?"

"It's called *sage*. Strange thing, apparently it grows around outside. Did you know that?"

"..."

The usage of drugs is fundamental to Academy City's Ability Development. Medicinal knowledge began to flow into his mind like a historical timeline.

Sage—a perennial plant of the Lamiales order, native to places on the Mediterranean Sea. Its leaves are called salvia. In addition to its medicinal usage, it is also cultivated as a spice and as a decoration... That was about all he had.

"So what are you gonna do with some herbs? Chomp down on 'em to recover your HP?"

"'Eich pee?'" Index angled her head. "I don't really understand that mysterious language you keep using, but sage is used for purification. I am about to use it to drive away the fleas all witchcraft-like."

"...I've got a really bad feeling about that. Are you going to feed those leaves to the cat? Or are you feeding them to the fleas?"

"Urk. I'm going to light the sage on fire and fumigate Sphinx with smoke to drive them away."

" ....
.... "

"I have enough common sense not to burn stuff inside the room!"

" ....
.... "

Kamijou looked at Index's face—her super-serious, super-sincere, and super-straight face.

Well, fleas are living creatures, too, so I can understand them hating smoke...I get that, but...

Then Himegami clapped her hands together in an exceedingly carefree manner.

"Don't be quiet. That's where you butt in. At this rate. A yummy herbal steaming of the cat will be ready soon."

Kamijou had felt his awareness sinking into the depths of the sea, but he resurfaced at what the priestess said.

"...Ah! Yes, right! Don't you know what the scariest part of a fire is, Index? If you cover the cat with smoke to get rid of the fleas, the cat will die along with them!"

Thank goodness Himegami is normal, he thought, relieved from the bottom of his heart. In the meantime, Himegami reached a hand into the sleeve of her shrine maiden clothing and began rustling around for something.

"...Hey, wait, Himegami. In the meantime, what are you taking out of *your* sleeve?"

"Hm? If you must ask. I must answer that it is a magical spray."

No matter how he looked at it, he only saw a bottle of pesticides.

" ....
Umm. What are you doing with...that?"

"I'm just going to point the magic spray at the vermin. And spray it."

"...Like I said, the cat is a living being just like fleas are, so don't bring out some Academy City experimental two-second cockroach killer! Would *you* immediately spray your face with bug killer if a fly landed on your face?!"

The two of them looked at each other with a "?" kind of face, and if Kamijou's hands weren't full, he'd probably have buried his face in them. What was so difficult, one might ask? The two of them were going to do these things because they were *honestly worried* about the cat, *that's* what was so tough.

Suddenly, Little Misaka, who'd been silent until now, opened her mouth to speak.

"If we are to be exchanging opinions on this, would it not be more effective to do so after putting down this juice? Misaka suggests, her arms full."

"Hm? Oh, right. Let's just put them down on the floor. Sorry. As thanks, I'll give you one you like, if you want."

"It's not necessary, Misaka responds. Then I will begin placing them on the floor. The seventh story is quite high up, so please be careful not to drop any to the ground, Misaka cautions, continuing her work."

Little Misaka's movements, logically consistent and evocative of a top-class sommelier, caused Index's and Himegami's own movements to come to a halt. They looked somehow shocked, in contrast to their usual troublemaking selves.

"...Wow. Touma, Touma. She looks just like a maid of honor at Windsor Castle."

"...She might bear a close resemblance. To the robotic maid projects from ages past."

Little Misaka didn't twitch an eyebrow at what they said.

"And now, as for what approach to take with that cat—"

"Whoa, nice job ignoring them...Or, I mean, you got an idea?"

"—It's not so much an 'idea,' but I recommend the simple usage of a commercial flea remover, Misaka offers. There should be a variety that is powdered medicine, and by spreading it onto the cat's body surface, the fleas will fall off."

"...Hmm, but it's still medicine. Couldn't that be harmful?"

Some might think it odd that a student of Academy City would say that—the city included the administration of drugs in its Curricula—but no matter what one thought, this kitten wasn't even a year old. The standards of "harmful" and "benign" medicines are different for an esper, since espers have built up an immunity to medicines over many years.

However, Little Misaka didn't seem to be paying it any consideration (though she never had an expression to begin with). "There is no medicine in this world that is not harmful, Misaka replies immediately and confidently. Between the detriment of the fleas and that of medicine, the former is likely more severe, Misaka supplies."

"..."

"The harm caused by pests like fleas and ticks is not something that ends with a simple case of dermatitis, adds Misaka. In the worst case, they could possibly be the trigger to create an allergic reaction severe enough to endanger its life, Misaka fears."

"Mgh," Kamijou grunted, falling silent.

Well, people do say that overusing cold medicine is linked to decreased immune levels, but when you're having nightmares because of a forty-degree fever, there's no choice but to take some...I mean, I understand it logically, but when I look at that cat, rolling around all over the floor like that, there's something illogical that I can't accept for some reason. Well, of course, it rolling about like that is an act taken to rid itself of the fleas on its body as soon as possible, I suppose...

Isn't there any way to do this without using medicine? He folded his hands, little healthy thoughts sprouting in his mind, when Little Misaka abruptly spoke.

"The idea is to get rid of the fleas from the cat's body surface without using medicine, correct? Misaka confirms. Of course, under the condition we do not use smoke or pesticides."

"...Look, I don't think either of them is doing any of this out of some malicious intent."

"If anything, them being without malice means they are beyond salvation, Misaka replies with an astonished look," Little Misaka answered, still completely expressionless. "In any case, you are the one who needs to supervise those two, Misaka warns. If you do not remove those girls from the cat immediately, I have a feeling property damage laws may be applied to this case, Misaka goes ahead and adds."

"...Which reminds me...Legally, were the lives of animals treated as property? That kinda sucks." Kamijou thought, half-seriously, that they should just make new laws for it. "Anyway, back to the topic at hand. Then, of course rejecting crazy ideas like smoke or pesticides, how would Little Misaka get rid of the fleas?"

The nun and the shrine maiden's shoulders twitched in unison.

"I see. Touma is going to rely on the girl he just met instead of me. I see, I see."

"Like this. The older characters disappear. Ha-ha-ha. We really are beyond salvation."

"..."

Kamijou decided to just ignore them already.

Looking at his drawn face, Little Misaka mentioned, still without expression, "I will ask once more. The point is to get rid of the fleas on the surface of the cat's body without resorting to pesticides or smoke and also without relying on medicine, correct? Misaka confirms one final time."

"Well, yeah, but how?"

"Like this, Misaka answers immediately."

Little Misaka waved the palm of her hand toward the balled-up calico.

In that moment, the sound of static electricity surging out of her hand exploded. The corpses of fleas fell from the cat's fur as if it had shaken off sand and sprinkled it all over. Sphinx's hair bristled and it bounced around, struggling—and just before it dove off the seventh story, Himegami caught it by the neck.

"I have destroyed only the fleas by using a specific frequency, Misaka reports. This type of insect repellent is sold normally at major volume sellers, so it should be safe and smooth."

She glanced at the door. "For inside the room, I believe that by using a smoke-emitting type of pesticide, you should be able to exterminate them easily, Misaka offers."

"Now then, if we are done here—" She turned her back and began to walk away without waiting for any thanks.

Index watched her back as it retreated, then finally said briefly, "Touma, Touma. I think that is exactly what a 'perfect and cool beauty' is."

Taking the opportunity, Touma interjected with equal brevity:

"I know I'm *really* asking for it here, but do you think you could please learn a little something from her?"

CHAPTER 2

Radio Noise
Level2(Product_Model)

1

He had remedial classes the next day, too.

Being a lone student, sitting in the middle of a classroom soaked in the afternoon sunlight, conjured up sadness within him. At the beginning, Kamijou was making sarcastic remarks like, "Wow, I must be in some village elementary school where you can clearly see the country's declining population!" Unfortunately, and as he thought it would, the novelty had worn off after this had continued for three or four days. By the fifth and sixth, the only feelings left within him were those of tedium.

However, there were only two more days of makeup classes, including today. He wasn't too far from the desperate mood of "yeah, my vacation finally starts on August twenty-second!" But he was still happy he'd be liberated from this.

He looked at the podium directly in front of him.

There stood his female teacher, Komoe Tsukuyomi. She was 135 centimeters tall and at a glance looked only twelve years old; only her face was peeking above the podium. She was reading out of a textbook atop it. *But wouldn't it be a lot easier to read if you held it in your hands?* he pondered.

"Now for the requisites for the ESP Card trials reenacted in the

United States in 1992. The materials for the card changed from vinyl resin to ABS resin. This was in response to a trick whereby rubbing finger grease, your fingerprints, onto the front of the card, you could make it so you couldn't tell what kind of card it was when it was flipped over— Wait, Kami, are you actually listening to me?"

"...Well, Miss Komoe, I'm listening and everything, but...Does this have something to do with our powers?"

Kamijou was a Level Zero Impotent.

Machines of the finest workmanship had measured him and given the results: that he couldn't bend a spoon even if he strained his head's blood vessels to their bursting point. And yet he had to go to remedial classes because his "powers" were weak. He couldn't make heads or tails of that.

Then Miss Komoe's lips turned into a frown, as if she had noticed that contradiction as well.

"But, but! If you give up because you say you have no power, then you won't be able to make any progress. So first you should start with the basics and learn where these powers come from. Then maybe you can discover how to bring out your very own power. That's what Miss Komoe thinks personally."

"Miss Komoe."

"Yeess?"

"...You look like you're pushing yourself, but it seems to me there's no progress to be made in the first place."

"Kami! I won't tell you that you'll succeed just as long as you put effort into it, but those who don't put any effort into it will never know success! Even Miss Misaka from Tokiwadai Middle School, who ranks third out of all 2.3 million people here, started out as a Level One Deficient. But she tried her best and then some and was able to reach Level Five! So, Kami, you have to try your best, too!"

"...*She's* number three? But she delivers roundhouses to vending machines!"

"? Kami, are you acquainted with Miss Misaka?"

"Not particularly. Back to the conversation, Miss Komoe, but Kamijou isn't someone who can get it going with this. You might

as well tell me, 'Look, this high school baseball player is so active, but despite being the same age, you're so lazy; don't you think it's disgraceful?' like I'm watching TV or something! Blech!"

"Please don't blech! You'll make Miss Komoe distressed, too!"

"Is that so? Miss Komoe, if you're so distressed, why does your face look so happy?"

"Eh, ah...well, that's...You see, it's because your teacher...She loves—"

"Ack?!"

"—her classes, okay?"

"...Ah, right. Your classes. That surprised me...Wait, hey! I went through all that to deflect the topic and make pointless conversation, and you just went back to the main topic on me!"

"A-ha-ha. It's a hundred years too soon for you to try and take on Miss Komoe with gum-smacking techniques. Here, Kami, please read from page 182 of your textbook about the defensive thought walls of psychometers with regard to criminal investigation, okay?"

And today's remedial classes go by once again.

2

Thus, today's makeup classes ended again.

The time was 6:40 PM. Kamijou was walking lazily through the shopping district under the evening light. He had missed getting on the last train, which was set up to be perfectly timed with the end of school. The last trains and buses in Academy City were generally at six thirty to prevent students staying out late on the town. The policy of putting all the means of transportation to sleep then was apparently to suppress kids going out at night.

Just one more day. Still one more day? Anyway, it's been a long time coming...Damn it, when it's over, I'm going to the beach or something! thought Kamijou as he headed back home in the sunset. It didn't look like the wind was blowing, but the propellers on the wind generators were spinning around and around.

"Hm?"

Then he spotted the back of someone he knew in the midst of the crowd of people. A brown-haired girl wearing Tokiwadai Middle School's summer uniform—it was Mikoto Misaka.

Well, no reason for me to avoid her. Kamijou trotted a bit and came up alongside her.

"Heya. You just getting out of makeup classes, too?"

"Eh?" Mikoto responded in an unfeminine way. "Oh, it's you. I'm tired today, and I was going to preserve the strength I had left, so I'll let you off the hook with the buzzy stuff today. What did you need?"

"Well, I didn't really need anything…We're going the same way, so I just figured I wanted to go home with you."

"Is that right?" Her eyes narrowed just slightly. "You're telling a lady of Tokiwadai that you 'just figured you wanted to walk back home' with her? Hah, do you have any idea how many men have worked their asses off to stand where you are now?"

"…Man, ladies who act like princesses are the worst."

"It was a joke, stupid," she retorted, sticking out her tongue. "The important part isn't what school you go to, but what you learn there. I'm mature enough to at least know that."

"Hum. I guess everyone has their own theories. Anyway, is your little sister not with you? She helped carry all that juice back yesterday, so I was sort of thinking I'd like to thank her."

Mikoto's eyebrow gave a twitch.

The movement was only a few millimeters, but those few millimeters oddly bothered Kamijou.

"My little sister…Did you meet her again after that?"

"Uh…"

Bad, thought Kamijou. She *had* grabbed Little Misaka's hand and forced her away from him yesterday. With that in mind, wouldn't it have been a better idea to have kept their second meeting a secret?

She narrowed her eyes again a little.

"What. Maybe you can't get my little sister out of that head of yours?"

"That's not it! She helped carry those cans back, so I just wanted to thank—"

"So even though we're visually the same, you'd still choose my little sister? Or maybe you couldn't decide, and you were trying to purchase a set of twin sisters?"

"I'm telling you, that isn't what I'm saying! Where did you learn that stuff, anyway?!"

Kamijou and Mikoto walked down the main road, bickering with each other all the while.

Many wind turbines stood on this main road. He raised his eyes above their rotating propeller blades and saw a blimp floating through the evening sky. The wide screen plastered onto it was displaying today's Academy City news, about how there had been three consecutive incidents in the past two weeks where agencies related to muscular dystrophy had announced their withdrawals and a cold wind blowing through the entire market was feared.

The conversation came to a halt, perhaps because his focus had turned to the blimp.

The word *blimp* might sound like it comes from ages past, but it was apparently a fuelless, eco-friendly aircraft that ran on solar power, generated lift via heating carbon gas inside the ship with a heater, and gained propulsion through the turning of giant motors.

If they're seriously developing stuff like that, then I wonder if we're really gonna hit the bottom of the planet's fossil fuels soon, he thought to himself like it wasn't related to him.

Mikoto remarked, "I really hate that blimp, you know."

"Huh? Why?" asked Kamijou, looking up at it again. If he recalled correctly, the Academy City Unified Board of Directors had put it up there in order to make the students more informed about current events.

"...Because people are following policies decided on by machines, that's why," she answered quietly, like she was spitting out something annoying.

He looked back at her again, at a loss. There was nothing weird about her face. Nothing was strange about it. It was sort of like she had made it back up before he saw a ruined clay mask.

"Yeah? What was it? Er, the Tree Diagram, was that what it was called? Hah, are you the type who can't stand how humans lose to machines at chess?"

Simply, the Tree Diagram was the smartest supercomputer in the world. It was the ultimate predictive simulator created under the pretenses of delivering more perfect weather forecasts.

The words *weather forecast* may seem familiar. In reality, though, the field is one in which you can forecast the weather but not state it positively. This is because the movements of each and every particle in the air that create the weather display these complexities, which involve things like the butterfly effect and chaos theory. So even if you can say that there's an 80 percent chance of it raining tomorrow, you cannot assert that rain will definitely be falling at precisely 9:10 AM. This concept is similar to quantum mechanics.

However, the Tree Diagram evolved these weather forecasts into weather *prophecies*.

It didn't do anything complicated. All it needed to do is predict the motion of every particle in the air floating through the world, and it could arrive at a singular answer.

It had some whacked-out specs, but according to one theory, the Tree Diagram's usage as a weather forecaster was actually a front, and that the goal was to use it for some other purpose.

For instance, there was just one irregularity in its forecasting.

It forecast the weather for the next month all at once.

It was still never wrong, so there wasn't any problem with it doing so. Frankly, he thought that was pointless effort. One might understand if they considered how overwhelmingly easier it is to get the next week's weather wrong than the next day's. If one wanted to accurately know the weather, repeating the calculation each day would make it go more smoothly.

But despite that, the Tree Diagram specifically chose a more difficult method, relying on its processing power.

Incidentally, according to rumors...

Apparently the time left over was being utilized for simulating calculations for research.

Drug responses, physiological responses, electron reactions—they would have the Tree Diagram calculate all of these, then after confirming the answer it spit out with two or three trials, they would complete a new medicine. It was pretty crazy. Talk was that there were even researchers who hated touching lab rats and didn't know how to handle a test tube.

A supercomputer possessing such immense power had its share of enemies, as well. Nobody knew when machine-hating human supremacists would commit a terrorist attack. Human-hating electronic supremacists could also try and sneak into the Tree Diagram's storeroom to steal the technology.

For all of these reasons, the Tree Diagram was installed in a place unreachable by human hands in order to protect against external foes.

To make it blunt, the man-made satellite shot up by Academy City was the Tree Diagram itself.

Rocket technology was not originally permitted to be developed by anyone but national agencies. And yet, it was being used privately in a place like this—it spoke to the depth of the influence Academy City had against the world.

Well, on the other hand, it's valuable enough for someone to let something so crazy pass, I suppose, mused Kamijou, staring vaguely up into the evening sky. Even now, the Tree Diagram might be calculating the end of the world from outside the atmosphere.

"A steel brain looking down on humans from the sky, huh? But it's not like it could possibly turn on humans, right? This isn't some cheap science fiction movie. When all's said and done, it's the same thing as an ATM—it just does whatever buttons someone presses on it."

Right. However much calculating capacity it had, the Tree Diagram can't operate without human intervention in the first place. An ATM destroying someone isn't due to machines rising up in rebellion, it's just that it's being used in an unplanned way by humans—same thing.

"…" Mikoto didn't respond. She looked up at the night sky one last time. Was she watching the blimp? Were her eyes piercing to something farther away? Kamijou didn't know.

"The Tree Diagram…loaded onto the man-made satellite *Orihime 1* and launched above Academy City under the pretense of analyzing weather pattern data—identified as the world's greatest supercomputer, to which no one will be able to catch up for another twenty-five years…," she said, as if rolling it around in her mouth, as if reading from an Academy City pamphlet. "…That's what they say, but I wonder. Does such a ridiculous absolute simulator even exist at all?"

"Huh?" Kamijou looked at her again, but she continued.

"Just kidding! Ah, I turned into a bit of a poet, aha-ha-ha!!"

Whoosh. She karate chopped him for no reason.

When he looked at her, he saw only brisk, impertinent, selfish Mikoto Misaka.

"Ow! What the heck did you do that for?!"

"Man, don't you have any dreams? You've never thought about dramatic friendship between a person and a high-tech sci-fi computer with a human heart? Nothing romantic like that?"

"Listen here, you…"

"Like a fighting maid robot or something."

"Listen to me! Wait, there's no romance in that or dramatic friendship, either! Are you even really a proper lady?! Aren't you supposed to be reading romance novels with a cup of tea in one hand?!"

"Whaaat? Quit that. What era of golden idols did you take that from? Every week on Monday and Wednesday I go to the convenience store and stand there reading manga! I mean, I'm only human!"

"Buy it! Also, you're bothering people around you!"

Without regard for Kamijou's declaration, she said, "I'm this way, see ya," and left immediately. He stared at Mikoto's back. Her mood was entirely different from a moment ago. He tilted his head and wondered…

…*I just don't get it. Is that just that thing where puberty makes you…Would it even be okay to say that? Maybe she just hates me.*

3

Given all of that, however, he couldn't figure out what he was looking at.

...That's Mikoto, isn't it? What's she doing?

Kamijou had parted with Mikoto, and after walking down the road a bit, he saw Mikoto crouched at the roadside. She was directly below a wind turbine, and there was a cardboard box placed at the foot of its post. *This is bad, I've seen this somewhere before.* His brain began to blare warnings at him at the same time he saw a black cat buried in the box.

Was she trying to feed it? She was slowly moving a sweet bun in her hand toward it, but the terrified cat had its ears lowered and was curled up as if she was waving her fist at it.

??? She went a different way and left me because she doesn't like me, right? So why is she right down the road? There's no reason for her to get here before me.

Once the question marks in his head stopped flying around, he finally caught on. At Mikoto's squatting feet was a pair of what looked like night-vision goggles.

It wasn't Mikoto—it was Little Misaka, who looked just like her.

"...Boy, without the goggles, I really can't tell them apart," Kamijou remarked to himself. Still looking at the black cat without expression, Little Misaka came to a halt. With not a single word, her neck turned like a lighthouse to face him.

"Heya. Just wanted to say thanks for the juice and the fleas from yesterday."

"...I am not particularly out for gratitude, responds Misaka."

With a hint of annoyance creeping into her inscrutable face, she slung the goggles on the ground over her forehead. She also withdrew the hand holding the sweet bun.

"The only reason I removed my goggles was to be in accordance with previously obtained information that cats possess a dislike of shining things like lenses, Misaka explains. Perhaps I need to apologize for making you mistake me for Big Sister?"

As she spoke, she hid the sweet bun behind her hand for some reason, her face still impassive.

For a cat who had been so afraid until now, it began to mew discontentedly.

Kamijou's head dropped to one side with a "?".

"If I made you apologize for something stupid like that, everyone in the world would demand an apology from me, I think," he sighed. "But if cats don't like lenses, then why did you put your goggles back on? What, did you not personally want to be seen like that?"

Indeed, it was hard to tell, what with the tranquillity of her wooden movements. Kamijou at least thought he saw her put them back on out of nervousness at being seen without him.

"...Not really, answers Misaka." Her voice came back to him immediately, but her expression was somehow misted over.

Kamijou tilted his head with a "?" again. Little Misaka, deadpan and dispassionate, had taken off her goggles so as not to scare the kitten and had crouched and beckoned to it with a sweet bun in one hand. It was certainly far from her normal image, but he didn't think it was really something she needed to hide.

"Then why don't you just give it the sweet bun? Cats don't hate them, do they?"

"No...That isn't really..." Her motions jerked to a stop. "Whatever the case, Misaka feeding this cat is most likely impossible, Misaka says in conclusion. Because Misaka has one fatal flaw, she adds."

"Don't call it a *flaw*, it makes it sound bad."

"No, the word *flaw* is appropriate. Misaka's body generates a weak electric field, explains Misaka. It is too weak for human bodies to sense, but as it appears, it is different for other creatures."

"???"

"Animals exhibit odd behaviors believed to be precursors to earthquakes. Many say this is also because they are responding to changes in electrical fields created by the planet's subterranean tectonic movements, Misaka explains in layman's terms."

"...Hmm. I suppose that means animals run away because they dislike it, then. In other words, animals don't find you likable because of the electric field?"

A tinge of irritation came over Little Misaka's face.

"I am not being disliked. I believe I am just not good with them, corrects Misaka."

"..."

This made him feel bad, so Kamijou decided not to press any further. Little Misaka peered at the black cat with placid eyes, hated by all animals because of her body's electric field. He sensed that he might be getting in the way here, then went to sneak away, but...

"Wait, Misaka calls, encouraging him to stop."

"Whoa! She caught me by just my aura!"

"Listen. There is one black cat here, Misaka says, pointing out the contents of the cardboard box. Do you really mean to leave without giving this hungry black cat anything? questions Misaka."

"...Wait, why do I have to be the one to pay for its snacks when you're the one trying to make friends with it? Besides, you've got a sweet bun in your hand right there!"

"I was not referring to that. There is an abandoned kitten here— why is it that you do not consider adopting it? Misaka demands again. Do you know what happens to animals collected by those from public health centers? Misaka says, launching into an allegory. First, they put the animal inside a transparent polycarbonate case, and then they inject into the box twenty milliliters of ADS10, a poisonous gas—"

"Wah!" Kamijou shouted loudly, cutting her off.

This conversation was incredibly awkward, especially given the fact that he was looking at a frightened cat.

"You adopt it! You found it, and you were feeding it, too!" Kamijou cried out as if it was obvious, but...

"...It is impossible for Misaka to raise this cat, admits Misaka.

Misaka's living environment is remarkably different from yours, explains Misaka."

Maybe her dorm's got strict policies, he thought. But his own residence hall didn't permit keeping pets, either. As someone who generally had zero intent to follow rules he didn't know the reasons for, it seemed weird to him that Little Misaka would give up on the black cat just for that, but...

She was crouching and just staring intently at it.

Her expressionless eyes followed the black cat, despite knowing that it would never get attached to her.

"...Wow."

Kamijou stopped walking in spite of himself.

He had been worried about this from the beginning, ever since he had adopted the first one—that adopting one would lead to adopting another, which would lead to picking up a third and even a fourth. Of course, though, the wallet of the Kamijou residence wasn't nearly fat enough to build an entire animal kingdom.

He wanted to refuse if he could. Unfortunately, he felt like Little Misaka would just stare at the black cat until morning if he let them be. She could even get into a fight with the people from the public health center.

"D-damn it...! Wasn't this the same exact thing that happened before?!"

"I find it impossible to understand what you are saying, but does this mean you possess the intention to adopt this black cat? Misaka inquires. In the case that you do not, employees from the public health center will—"

"Ah, shit, I got it, I got it, so stop staring up at me with those empty eyes and talking about public health centers!"

We've got rotten luck, you and me both, he thought to the timid black cat, gathering it up from the cardboard box into his hands.

"That's right, a name! This is your cat, after all, so take responsibility and name it!"

"...It's Misaka's?"

"Yes, it's yours." Kamijou looked down at the black cat in his

hands. It looked back up at him nervously. Little Misaka wasn't paying attention to them; her vacant eyes turned toward the night sky for just a moment, and she said...

"Dog."

"What?"

"I will name this black cat 'dog,' Misaka christens...Dog, even though it's a cat. Hee-hee."

Somehow, the sight of Little Misaka laughing quietly like she was remembering something was a little scary.

"...No, I mean. Think about it more seriously, please, since this is a living creature, and give it a more dignified name."

"Then, Ieyasu Tokugawa, reconsiders Misaka."

"Too dignified! Just wait, are you one of those characters who acts like she's thinking, but her mind is actually totally blank?!"

"Then, Schrödinger—"

"Stop doing that! A doctor who talked merrily about shoving a cat into a box spewing poison gas can't possibly have liked kittens, even if it *was* just a thought experiment!"

In the end, they decided to save naming the cat for later. However, it seemed to Kamijou that if they went on like this without deciding on one, it would be decided with a blunt name like "Later" or something, he thought, groaning.

4

The sky's color had resolved from orange into purple.

As Kamijou plodded along a main road, his gaze fell to the black cat in his arms.

He felt like he should figure out how to raise it now that he had decided in earnest to shelter pets.

...Well, it's only a little, but I do know a few things. Now, Index, on the other hand...

He sighed. The townscape he walked through was beginning to shift into the shades of nighttime. If they had been simple, mean-spirited pranks, he could just get rid of the mean-spirited bit.

Unfortunately, what Index did had been entirely out of good intentions; she thought it was the right thing to do. This put him in a most intractable situation. Her intent being wholly pure meant that she would stop and think about whether what she was doing was correct. He needed to run to the bookstore and buy a book on how to raise cats ASAP or else the beaming sister in white would soon come to be known under a different name: the cat killer.

"We are going in a different direction than yesterday, Misaka points out," said Little Misaka as she walked alongside him. Every time she stole a glance at the cat in his hands, he felt it somewhat unbearable. Cats didn't like her because of the electric field, but it seemed to him that she actually wanted to stroke the cat *really badly*, and she was just considering its feelings over her own and suppressing it.

"Uhh, just a side trip, that's all. There's a book I sort of wanted."

"Your objective is to go to the bookstore? asks Misaka. Geographically speaking, it might have been quicker if we had taken a right turn at the previous intersection, says Misaka, looking behind her."

"Urk. Not the store for new books—the used bookstore down a little farther. New or used, won't make a difference, right?"

"A hundred yen for a book would be ideal," he answered.

...Incidentally, unbeknownst to Kamijou, knowledge and common sense about living beings changes by the hour. Take the training routines for baseball players, for example. Ten years ago, a book might have this written in it like it was perfectly normal: "Q: How can I throw the ball faster? A: If you throw it harder, it will go faster. Even if it starts to hurt, just battle through it." If this were actually put into practice, it would surely ruin someone's shoulder joints.

"You are looking for a publication regarding the raising of cats? probes Misaka."

"Not really a publication, just some info. Besides, you saw those things in the nun clothes and shrine maiden outfit before, didn't you?"

"..." Little Misaka looked at Kamijou impassively. "I will say this again. Treat the cat's life carelessly and you will be tried for property damage, warns Misaka."

"Ah, huh? Wait, are you mad?"

"I am not mad. This is not something you can get away with just because you say you weren't involved, Misaka says, urging caution. If you leave those two alone while knowing what they are doing, that places responsibility on your shoulders as well, Misaka offers objectively."

"...I'm sorry. Little Misaka, are you mad?"

"I am not mad. In the first place, this isn't a case where the absence from the law makes it okay, Misaka admonishes you. Thinking about this sensibly—"

"Uhh..." He swallowed the urge to whine about how sick and tired he was of this. "Anyway, it'll be fine. After all, Index and Himegami are both only doing what they think is good for the cat. They won't inflict harm on it, or torture it, or do anything that they would clearly think is bad for it."

"As far as I can see from the situation yesterday, the level of trust I can assign to your words is incredibly close to zero, Misaka responds. And besides, how do you plan on dealing with it if the book has something mistaken in it? I believe Misaka should advise you, as she knows how to handle ca—"

"Aaahh!" Kamijou didn't listen until the end. "I'm telling you, it'll be fine! They won't inflict harm on it or torture it! They wouldn't do anything they would clearly think is bad for the cat!"

"...I have the feeling you are only repeating yourself word for word, the only difference being the tension in your voice, Misaka says, offering her thoughts. That wasn't my request—what I meant was, Misaka is—"

"Abgha!" He had no idea what was going on anymore. "I'b tebbing you it'b be bine! Inbex anb Hibebami are both onby boing bat they bink is bood for the bat abter all! They bon't inflibt barm on it or borbure it or anything that they boulb clearby bink ib bad bor it!"

"...———Grr."

"Hah...hah...oh, there's the bookstore! There it is!"

While he had been going on like that, they had meanwhile arrived at a big used bookstore chain. Kamijou looked down at the black cat in his arms and pondered it for a moment.

"Hm. Now that I think of it, I wonder if I should take the cat inside."

"That was a clear breach of the required level of explanation, but please refrain from entrusting it to me, Misaka says, seizing the initiative."

"...Why, because cats don't like you because of the electrical field your body puts out? Well, then. It looks like it's a wall you're gonna need to climb over in order to give birth to true friendship, now, isn't it? Take this—Killer Cat Boooomb!"

Kamijou turned sideways to face Little Misaka and, predicting she would catch it, slowly tossed the black cat at her. Of course, it was a foregone conclusion that the cat would land beautifully even if she didn't catch it, given its reflexes and mobility...Despite that, Little Misaka, just as Kamijou anticipated, reflexively held out her arms. How sad the nature of an animal enthusiast is.

Before Little Misaka could complain, Kamijou disappeared into the bookstore.

"...Good grief. Just what neural impulses approved the throwing of a kitten? Misaka grumbles to herself," grumbled Little Misaka, now standing alone in the Academy City sunset.

The black cat, reacting to the electromagnetic waves being released from her body, looked at her with frightened eyes. She considered lowering it onto the ground, but the cat hadn't accepted that Little Misaka and Kamijou were its "owners," so she got the feeling that if she took her hands off of it, it would run away forever.

The cat in question was merely a kitten, but there was no possible way a person could chase down a cat seriously trying to flee. But still, it was important that the first thing the owners needed to perform was to give it food, prepare a bed for it, and give it a sense of security, assuring it that it didn't need to run away from them.

"...And of all the things, he threw it, says Misaka, breathing a sigh," she said, her face completely blank. The silver lining was that the black cat wasn't baring its claws or particularly struggling around. It was probably more in the realm of *fear* than of obedience.

She certainly wanted to try touching the cat, even though it would be better to restrain herself if it was this scared of her...She sighed again...

...and then she noticed it.

It being summer break, boys and girls in casual wear were swarming the main streets of Academy City in the evening glow. Misaka's school uniform probably stood out quite a bit more than any of them.

But even so—she was completely ordinary compared to the boy she was looking at now.

It was a young man, whose hair and skin were both terrifyingly white. She didn't mean *white* as in "clean" or "innocent," but rather the polar opposite: white muddied with impurity. As if to further emphasize his rotting pallor, his clothes were collectively black.

And his eyes...

Red like fresh blood, crimson like a burning flame, scarlet like hell were those twin orbs embedded in his head.

He was far away amid the throng, and yet his very existence was astonishingly vivid. The boy wasn't doing something in particular. The boy was doing nothing exceptional, and yet...

If she ventured to say it, that hellish young man standing there was itself an abnormality in the middle of this peaceful city.

Accelerator.

The one extolled as the strongest Level Five in Academy City— and perhaps the strongest in the world—was simply watching Little Misaka. As he stared, he just smiled in silence.

"..."

She quietly lowered the black cat to the ground.

It will be killed. Anything with me will be caught up in the war and will surely be killed, I understand that. But it didn't leave her side. It trembled in distress but didn't run away; rather it looked up at her face as if its legs wouldn't move and meowed.

Accelerator regarded Little Misaka and grinned a grin far removed from the concept of "white"—a distorted, warped, corrupted, white-hot, cloudy, wrathful grin.

A single image passed through her mind.

A scene in the dead of night, an exploded Metal-eater ripping off a girl's right arm.

Little Misaka's ordinary life had ended at this moment.

From this moment on, her hell began.

5

The air-conditioned store was abound with boys and girls.

This was a location of a large used-bookstore chain. Aside from its low prices, it made sure you knew its policy of it being permissible to stand and read in the aisles. Many of the people here at the moment were the type who wanted to read manga, just not enough to purchase it.

"…"

Kamijou stood among them, aghast.

There was, in fact, a book called *How to Raise Cats* sitting right there on the bookshelf in front of him. Exposure to light had caused its cover slip to fade, but that made it even cheaper, so he wasn't about to complain.

But what's with this ordering scheme? he wondered.

Next to *How to Raise Cats* was a book called *Delicious Ways to Cook Beef.*

"…Okay, I guess they're both about animals, but still…"

Moving his eyes farther to the side in succession, he saw a book called *The Latest! Scientific Cows in Ranch Buildings.*

There were a handful of buildings in Academy City that didn't have any windows. Called "agricultural buildings," they were used for raising hydroponic vegetables and animals for consumption.

Inside the buildings, the vegetables, bathed in ultraviolet light, inhaled carbon dioxide passed through air purifiers and spread their roots into water fortified with all kinds of nutrients. When people outside of Academy City hear this, they apparently call it "gross." They appeared to think that scientifically created food was bad for their bodies.

...Even though it's the opposite. How can you possibly eat vegetables raised from soil when you don't even know what kind of industrial wastes and effluents were in it?

It's that kind of difference in values separating the inside of Academy City from the outside. Without giving it any more thought, he removed *How to Raise Cats* from the shelf.

She dashed around the back of the used bookstore into an alley.

One of her shoes slipped off.

Judging that it would be detrimental to her to run while wearing only one shoe, she took the other one off and left it behind as well, then pressed on.

At first glance, her brown hair cut to shoulder length, her white short-sleeved blouse, her summer sweater, and her pleated skirt would give her the impression of a Tokiwadai Middle School student. In addition, the name Mikoto Misaka might come to those who were familiar with her.

However, there were two things making it nonsensical to call her a middle school student.

One was the pair of army precision goggles sitting on her forehead. The other was the assault rifle she gripped in her right hand.

Though technically an assault rifle, it was made out of a laminated plastic rather than steel. Additionally, its form possessed a functional beauty reminiscent of a jet fighter. This would probably cause it to look like a toy gun that might appear in the world of science fiction. That analogy wasn't far off the mark.

The rifle, the F2000R Toy Soldier, would acquire its target via infrared light, and it was able to adjust the trajectory of its bullets in real time, using electronic controls, to give them the greatest chance of hitting the target. The wielder doesn't need to think about the direction of the wind or predicted evasion patterns of the target. All they needed to do was point the barrel in the direction this "thought-processing device" said to, and anyone could become an expert. In addition, thanks to the special impact-absorbing rubber enveloping the body of the gun and its carbon gas, the recoil from firing was nearly nonexistent. The antitank Metal-eater rifle was a monster that even grown men couldn't handle, but the F2000R, which had so little recoil it wouldn't even crack an egg, was a beast that even second graders could operate with ease.

In spite of having such a beast in her hands, she was nonetheless unable to take on the role of the pursuer.

Her raging pulse, her extremely irregular breathing, her thoughts blinking on and off again chaotically—all of these indicated exactly which one of them was the *hunted*.

A shadow approached her from the rear.

The pale boy drew to within just ten meters of her and said, "Hah-hah! Why ya runnin' away? You tryin' to seduce me by shakin' your ass all happy like that?!"

There was no place to run in this narrow, straight alley from someone wielding a gun, nor was there anywhere to hide—and yet, despite being unarmed, he was still reveling in the wild enthusiasm of the predator.

Without interrupting her flight, she twisted around her body from the waist to see behind her.

The muzzle of the F2000R she was holding at her hip sent its piercing gaze upon the pale boy, Accelerator, as if to freeze his hot midsummer's enthusiasm.

She didn't hesitate to pull the trigger.

The rifle quietly swallowed both the impact and the noise of it firing. With a minimal, sharply explosive sound like that of a cheap firecracker, it sent 5.56 mm bullets from its tip and drove them precisely into the boy's vitals.

Or rather, it should have.

"...?!"

Her body locked up in consternation. The 5.56 mm bullets boasted enough power to plunge through an entire automobile from one side to the other, but as soon as they struck the boy's body, they were repelled in every direction. It was as if she had fired a flimsy handgun at the front plating of an armored car.

Scritch. By the time she heard the sound of flesh being crushed, a reddish hole had already opened wide in her right shoulder.

One of the reflected bullets had lanced through it.

"...Eh...gh!"

Her body staggered. She immediately attempted to place a hand on the wall, but then her legs twisted and she rammed into the dirty concrete headfirst. She slid down the wall and collapsed to the ground.

"Hey, now, to kill some time, you wanna do a riddle or two? Okay, here you go: Exactly what did Accelerator just do, eh?!"

He laughed maniacally at her. When she looked up, the boy sprung one leg into the air, put all his weight behind it, and brought his foot down toward her skull to try and crush it.

"!"

She immediately rolled along the filthy ground to evade the incoming stomp. As she came out of the roll, she readied the F2000R, aimed up, and pulled the trigger.

She fired the stream of bullets from close range—there was essentially zero distance between them. The shells went precisely at the pale boy's eyes, to say nothing of his face. But again, the instant they made contact with his soft eyeballs, they bounced away.

The pale boy didn't even blink.

What came over that clouded face of his was a smile that looked like a hideous burn.

His white hand swept into the air. His hand—she hadn't a clue what effect it would have.

"...!"

She quickly hurled the now-empty F2000R at his face. She didn't think it would deal a mortal blow. She was only trying to create an opening for a moment so she could think of a plan.

But the boy still didn't move a muscle. The moment the body of the F2000R collided with his face, the gun shattered to pieces, like it had been chomped on by giant, invisible fangs.

She was astonished but had no time to pause to gape. Twisting herself around, she rolled, finally putting a step of distance between them. She waved her left hand around—it was the only one that would still move—gathered power into it, and…

…unleashed a spear of lightning.

The purple lance thrust forward at the speed of light. It should have had enough destructive force behind it to knock a person out.

She didn't think it would deal a mortal blow.

If she could just daze him and figure out a means of escape, that was enough.

But even so. Even despite that.

Of all the things that could have happened, the thundering javelin that crashed into the boy bounced back into her own chest.

"Gah…?!"

Thump! She fell to the ground with an impact that felt like a wooden hammer had been driven into her breast. Her breathing ceased, and all over, her muscles began to spasm.

She quickly managed one word from her trembling lips.

"Reflec…ted…?!"

"Nope, sorry! It's sort of like that, but my true nature is different!"

She tried to somehow get away from him. But because of the electricity she herself had launched, her body wasn't listening to a thing she told it.

"The answer is that I altered its *vector*! Momentum, heat, electricity…If any kind of vector so much as touches my skin, I can change it. Though I have it set on **reflect** by default!"

I don't believe it, she thought, looking up at him.

The 2.3 million espers living in Academy City were indeed special. However, those who could use their abilities to defeat a handgun were in the minority. If you could win against a handgun, then what about a machine gun? If you could win against a machine gun, what about a tank? What about a combat fighter? A battleship? A submarine? Ultimately, what about a nuclear missile?

There were no espers who could defeat something like that. The thing is, if you're going to go all the way through controlling someone's brain and changing their genetic makeup to create a power that can combat guns, then you could have just gone and bought a hand-gun or something. It's just a cheap weapon anybody could buy in a supermarket in the United States for thirty thousand yen. Going through all the legal loopholes and creating a large-scale Ability Development organization just for that? It would be ridiculous.

Therefore, Academy City's objective was not the espers. They were nothing more than the litmus paper in science experiments. The real treasure lies in why those espers are born and what the under-lying mechanisms are.

And yet, this boy stood out alone as different.

Motion, heat, current—he could alter the direction of anything, so even if an ultimate weapon, like a nuclear missile, were dropped on his head, he'd come out unharmed. Explosions that would mow down everything, high heat that would incinerate everything, neu-trons and radiation that would annihilate everything—he could reflect all of that.

The strongest Level Five in Academy City: Accelerator, the One-Way Road.

The term *behemoth* came to mind. This *creature* posing as a human being had the power to make an enemy of the entire world by himself and live through it.

He crouched at her side.

"A Level Five who controls all vectors, huh." It was so incredibly out of this world, but the boy spoke like it was nothing. "If I use it, I can do stuff like *this*, too, y'know?"

As he said that, he dug his slender index finger into the dark red hole in her right shoulder. His motion was akin to a child squashing a bug walking along the road.

"…!!"

Squelch, came a noise like an apple being split. Her body stiffened in extreme pain.

"Now then, here's a question for the loser struggling to turn the tables," the pale Accelerator said mockingly. "I'm touching 'blood' right now. I am touching the flow of blood. Now, if I take this vector, and I reverse the direction of the blood flow, what do you think will happen to the human body? If you get it correct, I'll put you to sleep nice and easy. ♪"

No sooner did her face go blank, presented with something she didn't know...

...than a pain exceeding all imagination assaulted her body.

"What's this?"

When Kamijou came out of the used bookstore with a shopping bag in one hand, he stopped in spite of himself and muttered.

Little Misaka should have been waiting here, but she was nowhere to be found. *Maybe she got angry at me forcing her to take care of the cat and left,* he wondered.

Only the black cat remained, sitting on the ground by itself.

Kamijou gathered up the cat, who was flopping its ears down and shivering somewhat, then took another look around. There was nothing particularly out of place on this road glistening in the sunset. There was just a lot of kids in casual clothing walking around, all heading back to their dorms after a day filled with fun.

......?

As he looked around, he inadvertently felt *something* coming from the ordinary scene. He swung around his head to get another look at things. There it was—an alley in the gap between the used bookstore and another building next to it. Something about it bothered him. *What is it? What exactly is getting to me?* he thought, taking a closer look. The entrance to the back alley bordered the tiled road, and nearby, the propellers of a wind turbine were spinning around and around, clattering all the while. There were a lot of leaves gathered from the roadside trees at the entrance, as if it was never really cleaned at all, along with a girl's shoe on the ground. The tiled road also broke off at the alley's entrance, and on the ground of the narrow passage was some pretty makeshift-looking asphalt—

—A girl's shoe?

"...?"

Still holding the black cat, he approached the entrance to the pathway. A bad omen slithered through his body like a bag of centipedes. A girl's shoe, just one, on the ground. It was a pretty school standard–looking, brown-colored loafer. The shoe wasn't especially dirty—in fact, it was fairly clean—which meant that not much time had passed since it was left there.

Kamijou stared into the path.

The sun was starting to set over the horizon already, so its light wasn't coming through the openings between buildings. He couldn't see anything farther down just by taking a little peek in. It was like a darkness, opening up into the entrance of a cave.

"..."

He took a step into the alley.

With but a simple motion, he thought he felt the temperature around him drop two or three degrees. The sensation of having tread upon the unknown rose from his feet and slowly up to the rest of his body.

He pressed on. There on the unkempt ground he found the other shoe. He advanced farther. His grim premonition swelled. *Slowly, slowly,* he thought, but his feet were rapidly speeding up. *What am I worried about?* he wondered, but his breathing and pulse were accelerating like he was falling down a hill.

Then he noticed markings on the wall, like something had cut into it. Marks like someone was shaving away the concrete with an iron nail. And it wasn't just one or two of them—the wall was scarred as if someone had been swinging a metal pole all over the place.

His feet stepped on something.

Golden metal...No, it was closer to the color of copper. It was a metallic tube about the size of a double-A battery. Kamijou saw that it was a bullet shell cartridge, the likes of which he'd never seen before except in movies. A smell, sort of like the smoky scent after fireworks, lingered faintly in the air.

What is...? Kamijou resisted giving voice to his unconscious thought. He proceeded deeper anyway, walking as quietly as he could for some reason. Every time he took a step, he got the weird sense that the air was getting dirtier.

When he plunged in a little deeper, he saw something sitting on the ground on the other side of this dimly lit place. No, to be more accurate, he saw someone lying on the ground. From here, he could see feet. He could see two feet. The rest of the body was invisible to him, swallowed up by the darkness ahead. Something was spread about around the feet. It was a mess of fragments, similar to plastic, and some sort of spring—like the wreckage of a toy.

"Misaka…?"

Why did her name come out first right then? Kamijou didn't know. He took another step forward, carving a path into the unseen.

There he saw her.

Little Misaka was lying there, reduced to a corpse.

6

She was faceup, eyes pointed overhead, to the square-shaped violet skies enclosed by the buildings.

There was a sea of blood. It was such an ocean it might make one doubt just how much blood was stored inside the human body. It wasn't only on the ground. Both walls had been splattered by a red pigment at a height about eye level with Kamijou. It looked almost as if someone had been squeezed like a sponge, like every last drop of blood had come out.

One girl was in the center of this crimson ground zero.

Her arms and legs, which extended from her short sleeves and skirt, had been torn off. It was more than likely the same story underneath her clothes. Her uniform was dyed with such vivid scarlet that you couldn't tell what color it originally was. Even though her whole body was ripped apart, however, there wasn't a modicum of damage on her clothing.

It was as if someone had fed a thin wire into all of her blood vessels and then dragged it back out again. Her body was ripped apart from the inside out along the flow of blood. The way her arms were cut open reminded him of science class frog dissections. Neither was there anything close to a "face" on her sundered form. Instead, like a flower in bloom, or perhaps like a boiled egg with its shell pulled off, there was only a dark red cavity, revealing bundles of pink muscle and yellow, gelatinous fat within.

"U...ah......"

Kamijou automatically took a step back from the red and violet scene. The black cat started meowing up at him painfully, as if he had started to crush it with his arms.

"A......gh..."

He had witnessed hell before. The hell was called Misawa Cram School. But the corpses he had seen then were all either covered in armor or melted into pure gold. The fact that they were flesh and blood had never truly set in.

But this was different.

The urge to vomit rose in his throat like he had shoved a finger down it. *Don't throw up!* Kamijou's mind roared. *Why the hell would you look at her and throw up? That's Little Misaka, you know!* Someplace in his brain was shouting rose-colored logic at him...and that's when he caught sight of Little Misaka's skirt.

Something was protruding from her skirt, from between her legs.

A thin layer of purple covered its pink surface, **and it was soft and spongy—**

"Uh, geh!"

That instant, Kamijou could endure it no longer, and he bent over. That sour taste spread into his mouth, and immediately after, the contents of his stomach all flew out.

He vomited.

That was someone who had been talking to him with a smile just ten minutes ago. The queer fact nearly burned out the cogs in his thoughts.

The vomit fell to the ground with a disgusting noise as it mingled with the edge of the pool of blood, creating an odd-looking marble pattern.

Blood.

With that, at last, he realized. The blood hadn't dried at all. Blood fluid coagulates in fifteen minutes—therefore, the person who did this ought to still be nearby.

The one who did this.

Kamijou blanched at his own words. Indeed, however he looked at this, it didn't seem like an accident or a suicide. His head was swimming. The only remaining possibility didn't want to manifest itself into words.

Just then...

Crumple. He heard some kind of noise coming from deeper in the alley.

"?!"

Ordinarily, he'd have assumed it could have just been a stray cat or something. But this sea of blood had already flown far beyond the category of common sense. His feet stepped back of their own accord. The darkness was indeed frightening, but the more important thing was that he couldn't even consider walking past Little Misaka like **this**.

One step, then another...As he withdrew, he recalled the solid sensation in his pocket. It was his cell phone. *I'll get help from someone,* he thought, *but then won't the danger come to me while they take their sweet time getting here? Even if I do get help, I need to get out of here first,* he concluded, turning his back to Little Misaka. He started to run away and retreated from the back road.

He had thought this alley was totally straight, but he slammed into the wall a few times as the ground beneath his feet rocked back and forth. He hit some buttons on his cell phone as he ran, but his fingers were shaking, so he didn't really know what he pressed. It might have been 110, it might have been 119, or maybe 117, or 177. Anyway, he pressed something. The ringtone sounded a few times, and then he heard a *bzt* sound.

It finally went through! He braced, but all he heard from the other end was a cold electronic sound going *boop, boop.*

Kamijou took the phone away from his ear and looked at the screen.

He didn't have any reception. Suddenly, he really wanted to throw it.

*　　*　　*

Weird how inconvenient cell phones can be, huh? thought Kamijou in a daze.

He had used his phone to try and call for help, but it said that it had no signal in the narrow alley. With no other choice, he exited from the path and dialed 119 again, this time from in front of the used bookstore.

If someone were to ask what he said over the phone, he wouldn't be able to answer.

The only record of his crazy, nonsensical attempt at an explanation was recorded as an entry in his call history for the rare number 119.

On the main road was the hustle and bustle of normal, ordinary life. He didn't think anyone would believe it if he told them there was a destroyed girl's corpse lying on the ground just a few steps into that alley.

"…"

His gaze fell to the cell phone in his hand.

In all honesty, he needed to let Mikoto know, too. Unfortunately, he didn't know her cell phone number. Even that one small thing was beyond his ability at the moment, and it made him feel enormously helpless.

The black cat in Kamijou's arms yawned.

He had called 119, but the police had come along instead.

His biological clock was beginning to go astray, so he didn't quite know how much time had elapsed since notifying them. He got the feeling it had been more than an hour, but at the same time, he felt like it had only been about ten seconds.

According to the screen on his cell phone, thirty minutes had passed.

At first he thought his phone was broken, but when he looked up at the sky, he found it had gone from purple to the deep blue of night. He blankly stared at the light from the twinkling stars.

"…"

He quietly watched the police's arrival.

To be more precise, they were Anti-Skills, not police. They weren't espers; they were more like soldiers armed with next-generation weaponry. It looked as if they were currently under the impression there had been a homicide by a berserk esper. Nearly ten Anti-Skills alighted from a windowless station wagon, each protected by a jet-black helmet and a suit made of special fiber—very robotic outfits. In their hands were these strange things that looked sort of like rifles. The equipment seemed to speak to their priority: capture the criminal, not defend the civilians.

"...You? Excuse me!"

An Anti-Skill suddenly addressed him as he sat there in a stupor. He twisted his head. *They only heard my voice, so they shouldn't know my face, right...?* But when he looked around, he saw that the Anti-Skills had spread out and were apparently calling on other people nearby, one after the other.

"Oh, I'm the one who notified you. Except I called for an ambulance, not the police..."

"Is that so? When there's an incident involving criminality, it's set up so the police naturally get notified as well. We probably arrived quicker than they did. Well then..." The Anti-Skill looked him in the eyes. "...The alley in question, is it that one? Also, could you tell us a little about what it's like inside right now? It would be a big help."

Kamijou shut his eyes once. What he had seen in the back alley was stuck to the backs of his eyelids like glue.

And he said, "...There's a person dead."

His voice was surprisingly calm, which annoyed him.

"The whole body was, like, torn to pieces...I don't know the weapon used or anything. I think it might have been some kind of *power.*"

With every word that came out of him, he felt more nauseous.

It was an unpleasant feeling. It felt like the sensation in his paralyzed body was returning.

"She was somebody I knew. I only met her two days ago, but if you showed me a picture of her, I'd know who it is. Ah, I don't...Why am

I staying this calm? I should be more distraught, right? So then, why, why am I…!"

"That's enough." The Anti-Skill shook her head a little. "You made the best choice. That's why we're here. It's not that you couldn't do anything."

"…I ran away, you know?"

"Still. You did good," replied the Anti-Skill.

Kamijou knew that these words were only temporary comfort. But those words were enough to hit his mental brakes. He just barely averted a complete breakdown.

"Normally we'd want the witness to come along with us, but do you want to? Looking at you, we can't seem to force you to, but…"

He felt a chill run up his spine when he heard that. His fingertips were on pins and needles, like the scape of flesh and blood and entrails was burned into his eyes.

"…I'll go," said Kamijou, black cat in his hands.

He didn't know why. He just didn't want to run away anymore.

Will I have to look at it again?

When Kamijou considered the prospect, he shivered. But he still had to go into that alley. What had *happened* in that darkness? There was no way he wasn't going to figure that out.

The fortified Anti-Skills took up positions to protect him, and he led them into the back alley.

…Huh?

As soon as he took one step into it, he felt like something was wrong.

The shoe wasn't there.

Yes, right at the start, Kamijou had seen one of a pair of ladies' loafers sitting at the entrance to the alley. And as he went deeper in, he saw the other one lying on the ground, hadn't he?

He turned back to look behind him. There was indeed a shoe plopped on the ground at the entrance.

But the second shoe, which should have been dropped farther down, **was nowhere to be found.**

...?

Kamijou felt a heavy weight drop into his gut, but the Anti-Skills rapidly pressed forward. Next there should be an empty cartridge on the path and marks on the wall. **Yes—there should have been.** And yet there was no cartridge. It looked like someone had come through and cleaned it. There wasn't a single thing on the filthy ground. The scratches on the wall had been sanded down by something. It couldn't erase the marks themselves, but it was enough to conceal what had made them. It was almost like somebody was desperately trying to hide them.

...*Wait a minute.*

Kamijou got a bad feeling about this. The pressure in his stomach dropped. He wanted to stop for a moment and think about this, but the Anti-Skills nevertheless progressed quickly. An eerie sensation struck him, like insects were crawling beneath his skin. The vanished loafer and cartridge. The clearly sanded-away marks on the wall. He got the feeling that these scattered words and phrases were giving way to a strange chemical reaction, attempting to coalesce into a singular meaning.

He wanted to stop for a moment. But he could not. His feet were dragged forward as if they were being pulled along by an invisible rope connected to the Anti-Skills.

Then they finally arrived.

Kamijou's breath stopped.

It was the site of the homicide—the entire ground covered in blood, and Little Misaka sinking into it, having passed away.

The corpse that should have been there was nowhere in sight.

7

It wasn't just the corpse that was missing.

In addition to the ground, even the crimson blood staining the walls at his left and right had vanished entirely, wiped away like it had been nothing more than dirt on glass. There wasn't any hair or any pieces of flesh scattered about anymore. He didn't smell blood in the air, either. Even the scent of flesh no longer remained. As if there wasn't any corpse here to begin with...as if there had been no incident in the first place.

"Eh?"

The first thing to escape from Kamijou's lips was a grunt of surprise.

He stopped, and the Anti-Skills in the lead turned back to look at him.

"What's wrong? Is there something bothering you?"

"No, not like that..." First, he pointed to the ground. "It's there. There was...supposed to be...a corpse there, but..."

"What?"

The Anti-Skills looked at the ground, but of course, there wasn't a single drop of blood, to say nothing of a dead body. There also weren't any particular signs of it having been cleaned up, nor were there traces of any stains.

They exchanged looks with one another through their helmets. A sour air came over them. Some of them relaxed their shoulders, and some were clearly glaring at Kamijou.

"W-wait a minute! There was seriously someone dead here!"

"I understand." One of the Anti-Skills looked at him. "If what you saw was real, then was it actually in this spot? Could you have gotten confused and mistaken it for a different place? Is that at all possible?"

His words were gentle, but they lacked seriousness, like a flat soda. Kamijou thought his tone sounded like one that you might use when comforting an excited, intractable drunk.

What happened...? He was at a loss.

Had it been just an illusion? If it was, then where did Little Misaka go? She should have been waiting in front of the bookstore. He took out his cell phone. The fastest way to discern whether it was some hallucination or the real thing was to simply call up Little Misaka and confirm. If the call went through fine, then Little Misaka was "alive."

But he hadn't the slightest clue what her cell phone number was. Making a call. He couldn't even perform that single task...The only option left for Kamijou was to guess on his own.

"..."

He stood frozen in that spot.

The scene before his eyes was in every way ordinary—enough so to make him doubt his very memories. And, in reality, **he was happier that his memories were the more doubtful.** If that was the case, then everything that had happened was just some sort of trick, and he gave the police a nonsensical notification about it. Little Misaka was walking lazily and aimlessly along somewhere totally different, and when she remembered the black cat, she'd appear before him again unexpectedly. Of course that future would have been much more preferable.

...Damn it. What's going on?

He was happier with thinking Little Misaka wasn't dead. Still, he felt a hesitation at rejecting the reality he had seen, playing it off as an illusion with scant few words. The queer contradiction started to gnaw at his heart.

"What the hell is going on here, damn it?!"

Eventually, he just couldn't deal with it anymore. He pushed aside the Anti-Skills and ran deeper into the alley. He heard their voices behind him, trying to get him to stop, but they probably wouldn't come chase him. They were already just about to put everything down to a prank call.

The cat in his hands offered a meow.

He ran through the dark passages without any idea what he was trying to find. Well, he was looking for *something*; he just didn't know what that *something* was. It partly seemed like the only reason for his run was to vent all the strange stuff he had pent up.

As he continued to dart down the dim, rotting alleyway, he came to a T-intersection. The path was split, going right and left. To the right was the same old, narrow passage continuing into the darkness, but in the other direction, he could see the lights of streetlamps shining. That way probably led to a main road. It seemed like light at the end of a tunnel.

His emotions imparted his desire to take the left path.

He thought, however, that leaving this back alley behind was the same as giving up. So he headed into the blackness to his right.

It got a bit wider here than before, just barely turning into a way rather than a path. On the other hand, there were buckets, abandoned bicycles, and other various things strewn about, perhaps because of the added space. All sorts of fluids were flowing out of knocked-over beer cases and cardboard boxes that looked like they'd absorbed water. They were all mixed and combined to form some kind of viscous liquid.

And in that liquid he saw what looked like footprints leading farther down the path.

Kamijou followed them with his eyes, and when he peered into the dark ahead, he saw something rustling.

Someone was there.

He froze. His heart nearly exploded with surprise.

The black cat started squirming around, distressed. All the nervousness might have caused him to tighten his hold on it.

"Who's there?!" he tried shouting, but he actually really did not know who they were.

Whoever was in the blackness noticed the voice and looked at him.

The person was unexpectedly shorter than he. It looked like a girl. However, there was something that looked like a sleeping bag slung over her shoulder, and it was really ominous. Yes, a sleeping bag. A bag meant for pushing someone unconscious into. The silhouette of that sleeping bag, bent over the person's shoulder like a fulcrum, looked like an exhausted, drained female.

What's...that...?

He couldn't help but stand dumbstruck at the oh-so-vivid silhouette. A living human was stuffed in there...Actually, it was more like a jumble of disassembled mannequin parts shoved in it. The form as a whole looked destroyed, but various pieces, like wrists and ankles, pushed out from the fabric in an oddly lifelike manner.

And Kamijou saw...

...that somebody, who had only been a shadow until now because they were in the darkness. The somebody, who had clearly been put into a sleeping bag.

Kamijou saw...

...that somebody, on the other side of the darkness, past the darkness that had now been rubbed away was...

Little Misaka.

"Wha...?"

Kamijou's motions came to a complete halt at what he saw. The black cat in his arms offered a friendly cry, which was rather strange, given the situation.

There was no doubt that she was Little Misaka.

Brown shoulder-length hair, with army goggles on the forehead... A short-sleeved white blouse with a summer sweater and a pleated skirt...There she stood, as if she had been repaired using a mold.

He didn't know what to think about this, but...

"I apologize. I planned to return once I completed my work, Misaka says, offering an apology to start off."

Her stare, her bearing, the air she exuded, her tone of voice—they all belonged to *her*, beyond a shadow of a doubt.

"Hey, hold on. You *are* Little Misaka, right?"

If she *was*, then was everything before actually just a realistic illusion? Dissatisfied as he was with that explanation, the figure of Little Misaka was nevertheless standing there, the same as she always was.

He sunk weakly to the ground.

"Damn it. Then what *was* all that?" spat Kamijou. "Ah, sorry. This might be a really sickening story to tell you in particular, but up until now, I thought you had gotten into something dangerous or something. It seems like you're fine, though. Thank goodness."

"...There are parts of what you say that I do not quite understand..."

Well, I suppose she wouldn't, thought Kamijou. *I don't really know why I had that sort of hallucination, but everything is okay if Little Misaka is fine, right?* he decided...

"...Misaka has died in all properness, reports Misaka."

Kamijou's breath stuck in his throat.

Little Misaka is in front of me. But now that she mentions it, what could be in that sleeping bag she has on her shoulder? he realized a bit late. It was like a broken mannequin had been thrown into it, since its shape implied that its joints were all facing in ways they shouldn't be.

What is in that sleeping bag? he puzzled, shifting his gaze to it. Then something leaped into his vision. Something had jutted out from the fasteners on the sleeping bag. Like a clump of grass, peeking out of the openings between the fasteners, was brown—

—hair.

He gasped as a nondescript chill surged through his body.

Is she carrying a realistic, life-sized doll? he thought. However, that brown hair was all too familiar. Yes—its color, its luster, everything about it was the exact same as the girl holding that sleeping bag.

"Wait...a second. What...are you carrying exactly? What the hell is in that sleeping bag?"

"...? You do not know? Misaka responds with a question. I had thought you were related to this experiment because you were present in the test area, but...I see. You certainly do appear to have little to do with the experiment, Misaka answers by intuition."

Experiment...?

Kamijou was quiet for a moment. He didn't understand her at all.

"Just to be sure, I will confirm with the password, Misaka says, as she promised. ZXC741ASD852QWE963, she tests."

"Wh...at? Hey, what have you been going on about?"

"As you cannot decode the password, it does not seem that you are a participant in this experiment, Misaka says, supplementing her intuition with evidence grounded in logic."

It might as well have been an alien language coming out of her mouth at this point.

He looked at her dubiously, but she continued.

"It's Sister inside this sleeping bag, Misaka answers."

Replying to his doubts was indeed Little Misaka's voice…

But, **from behind Little Misaka**, he heard a *clap* of footsteps approaching.

For some reason, the voice was coming from somewhere more distant than Little Misaka's. It was like it had reached him from farther down the alley.

And, in reality, Kamijou's sense was right on the mark. With only the *clip-clap* of footsteps, somebody was approaching Little Misaka from behind.

"I apologize for leaving the black cat behind, Misaka asserts."

The person who appeared out of the darkness—it was a girl who looked cut from the exact same mold as Little Misaka.

What? She has the same face as Little Misaka…Does that mean this one is Mikoto?

"However, I was not willing to drag an animal into unnecessary conflict, says Misaka, defending herself."

But he was wrong. There hadn't been just one set of footsteps.

"I'd like to apologize to you for all this as well, says Misaka, bowing her head."

Two, three, four, five, six, seven, eight, nine, ten—the number of unique sets of footsteps was increasing endlessly.

"It seems that we have caused you unnecessary worry because of the experiment, says—" "However, there is no need to fear—" "The fact that you called the police was also—" "A correct judgment—" "Is the black cat safe? asks—" "All of the Misakas here are Misaka, so—" "However, if I were really the killer, then what did you plan to do?—" "The details are confidential, so I cannot explain, but in any case, no crime was committed here, Misaka answers.—"

"...Wha?"

Kamijou automatically took a step back from the Misakas who were appearing one after the other. His back ran into something with a *thump*. He turned around to see more Misakas, with the exact same face, looking at him with that blank expression.

"What's...all this?"

As he stood face-to-face with this situation in bewilderment, he tried to make all the puzzle pieces fit together in his mind.

Was what he had seen no hallucination at all, then? Had one of the identical Misakas been killed? When he saw Little Misaka shouldering that corpse, it seemed also like she was trying to hide the body...

The truth is, if you use a coagulant and a hair dryer, you can harden blood in one minute easy. It was the same concept as solidifying tempura oil with chemicals in order to discard it. Plus, you can use a few solutions to erase fingerprints and luminol detections pretty simply.

He still thought something was odd, though.

From the start, the presence of so many people who looked exactly the same struck him as strange.

Identical twins—in other words twins who look the same—do indeed have the same skeletal structure, since they are equivalent at a genetic level. But the way it happened in dramas and novels, where the twins would have the exact same face, was a far cry from reality.

For example, say that there was a person named Tanaka. Depending on if Tanaka decided to train every day to become a baseball player, versus if he decided to screw it and eat candy all day, the layout of his muscles and fat would obviously be different.

Sleep, exercise, eating habits, stress—even if they were born at the same time, if the "rhythm" of one's lifestyle changes, that person's body would obviously change along with it. To add to that, people don't normally strive to ensure that their sleep, exercise, and eating habits align with each other to some kind of schedule.

In the face of that, the girls he was seeing looked way too alike.

They looked far too similar to one girl named Mikoto Misaka.

Their sleeping times measured by a clock, their amount of exercise dictated by a ruler, the quantity of food they ate weighed on a scale...

Yes, it was as if everything about Mikoto Misaka were being calculated by precise equipment, and all of them were being made to align with her actions.

Almost as if someone had created them.

"...
...."

Kamijou took a look around and then laid eyes upon the sleeping bag one more time.

It seemed like they knew him. It looked like they knew the black cat, too. But it would make even less sense if they did. Who was the Little Misaka he'd known until now? Was she in this crowd right now, or were there many more Misakas aside from her? Could the girl stuffed into that sleeping bag really be the Little Misaka he had been talki—

"Oh, you needn't worry, answers Misaka."

As he stood there, mouth agape, the one to address him this time was the Misaka shouldering the sleeping bag.

"The Misaka you have interacted with before now is serial number 10032—in other words, this Misaka, she responds." She motioned to herself with her free hand and continued. "Our brain waves are linked to one another by means of *Misaka's* ability to control electricity. This is all no more than the other Misakas sharing number 10032's memory, Misaka adds to her explanation."

Linked brain waves—this suddenly turned into an unbelievable story, but if they were twins, then it was possible. Like one's fingerprints and voice print, brain waves differed from person to person. Even if one tried streaming someone else's brain waves into their own, the only result would be a few cells getting destroyed. But if two people were genetically identical to each other...

Whatever, that doesn't matter, thought Kamijou.

He asked her who she was.

"We are the Sisters—somatic cell clones of our big sister, who is one of only seven Level Fives in Academy City—created for mass production in the military, answers Misaka."

He demanded to know what she was doing.

"Just an experiment, answers Misaka. Allow us to apologize to you once more for getting you involved in the latest trial, Misaka says, bowing her head."

He questioned...or rather, he was about to say something, but his mouth suddenly refused to work.

The girl in front of him was so extremely different and so incredibly distant.

Kamijou rested his back against the wall of the alley, alone, the black cat in his arms.

The multitude of Misakas had disappeared into the darkness. They were most likely bringing out the corpse and wiping off any and all worthwhile evidence. In addition, those "experiments" would continue. He didn't know what they were exactly, but they probably involved more Misakas being killed and their corpses being dragged away, all without anyone knowing.

He suddenly felt the urge to throw up at the words *somatic cell clones*. The spine of the book he had found by coincidence at the used bookstore floated back across his mind. *The Latest! Scientific Cows in Ranch Buildings.* They live their whole lives, breathing conditioned air and drinking nutrients in a building with no windows, raised for the sole purpose of being eaten. Their guts are cut open; their organs are dragged out; they're sliced into thin pieces, put into tray packs, and scattered around butcher shops and supermarkets throughout the city. *Ugh*...Kamijou felt the sour taste of stomach acid rising in the back of his throat. At the moment, he was seriously considering becoming a vegetarian.

However, there were many pragmatists in the world who didn't pay any heed to it. These were the kind of people who would do all that to humans—cut open their guts, drag out their organs, slice them into thin pieces, and put them into tray packs—and they would probably go on with these "experiments" without twitching an eyebrow. He didn't know what these experiments were all about. He didn't know if he'd understand it even if something this atrocious was explained to him. But there was one thing he could state for sure: The longer this experiment went on, the more lives would continue to be lost.

...*Experiment?*

Kamijou felt himself hung up on something about that.

Right, an experiment. Little Misaka had called it an *experiment*, hadn't she? Wouldn't that mean some research organization was behind it all? When he thought about it that way, the specialized term *somatic cell clones* made sense to him, too. Somatic cell clones weren't born in the same way as a baby. It was a human-creation method that involved extracting a person's genetic data from a single hair or drop of blood...and once he thought that far ahead, he paused.

A single hair.

Yes. A person would need genes, the raw materials, in order to make this kind of clone. It didn't matter whether it was a strand of hair or a bit of blood—one just needed that ingredient.

Little Misaka had told him they were mass-production, military-use models of Mikoto Misaka.

Could she have...?

Kamijou caught his breath. In spite of himself, he looked up at the sky, boxed into a square, at his hopeless notion.

Could Mikoto Misaka have known about this?

8

Tonight they were having *yakiniku*—grilled meat.

Miss Komoe, who looked twelve years old, gazed at the twelve-thousand-yen Splendid Yakiniku Set she had bought on sale at the supermarket. The number of people living here *had* increased, of course. It was also one rank above the eight-thousand-yen Beautiful Yakiniku Set she usually ate from.

Incidentally, there being more people residing here at the moment wasn't all that rare an occurrence for Miss Komoe. She was, at her core, an educator, so she made a "hobby" out of picking up runaway girls and giving them a temporary place to stay until they figured out what they wanted to do.

...The latest one, little Izanami, went to apprentice at a bread shop a month ago. Now that I stop and think about it, I've been living by myself for quite a while now, huh?

Miss Komoe removed a few different varieties of beer from her fridge so she could compare their tastes.

The particular seasonal affinity of *yakiniku* was unclear to her, because in this day and age, you can obtain any kind of food all year round.

But though she appeared only twelve, Miss Komoe was a teacher who knew her beers. For her, *yakiniku* was a decidedly summer dish. In fact, she decided that today, cooking the meat would be up to her roommate boarding here without paying rent. To state it bluntly, Miss Komoe was planning to drink beer and be served meat on long chopsticks tonight. In other words, she felt a bit like a queen.

Meanwhile, this roommate, Aisa Himegami, had finished preparing the hot plate. She was now performing a ceremony in front of the tea table positioned dead center in the room, one in which she sat in lotus position to kill the worldly desire called an *appetite*. The term *lotus position* may sound bombastic. All she was *really* doing was sitting cross-legged, enduring her empty stomach, and quelling her urge to ask if dinner was ready.

Miss Komoe was one of the people who seasoned her meat before cooking it.

Everyone has their own myriad preferences, but she loved the double structure of putting sauce on the meat before cooking it and then *again* afterward.

Of course, cooking meat with the sauce on it would be a disaster— the hot plate and the room would be filled with stench and smoke. She didn't mind it, though. The floor and walls in her room already, for some reason, had strange rune-like sketches drawn all over them; the tatami had been sliced by what seemed like a sword; there were bloodstains left all over the place; there were burn marks on the walls; and to top it all off, the walls and ceiling had been wrecked by what she could only surmise was some kind of beam weapon. It had been repaired with plywood for the time being, but her security deposit and compensation money were pretty screwed.

...Urr. Tomorrow for sure, I'll give Kami a good scolding and ask him what happened.

She heaved a sigh, but then collected herself and headed for the tea table with a large dish of meat in her hands. Himegami already had the rice cooker in her arms, implying she was one of the people who would drown her meat in sauce and eat it on rice.

"I'm going to turn on the hot plate, okay? Hime, you lost the game of rock-paper-scissors, so you're on slave labor duty. Get those serving chopsticks ready! Now then, please cook the meat lickety-split for Teacher~."

"Okay. But first. A scary story from Academy City."

"...It will take more than the seven wonders to make Miss Komoe cry. Besides, there are even opinions, dishonorable though they are, that Miss Komoe herself might be one of the seven wonders! So I'm totally okay and completely unconcerned, all right?"

The seven wonders were urban legends passed down in Academy City. However, they weren't the usual scary, occult ghost stories; they tended to be conspiracy theories of the government hiding the existence of UFOs or something.

The urban legends here, frankly, were mostly related to the talk of the town—the Imaginary Number School District, the Five Elements Society.

They say that everything that had happened in Academy City was the work of one single research institute. The company housing for employees, its recreational centers, and other related establishments are said to have kept on multiplying, at some point ballooning into one giant city.

But at the present time, no one knew where in the city the "institute that started it all" was.

There were plenty of rumors, though. For example, that the institute had gone bankrupt some ten years before, away from the eyes of people. For example, that it was hidden underground. For example, that you might see it every day, but it's camouflaged as a perfectly normal school. For example, that it was hidden in some sort of warped space made from a special ability or some fictional technology.

The seven wonders were rumors and had hundreds of variations depending on the storyteller, but every one of them was alike in that none had any kind of backing.

It was something that should, for all intents and purposes, *exist*, and yet no one noticed its presence.

Twenty-three school districts existed in Academy City, and the one that didn't fit into any of those numbers was...

The Imaginary Number School District or the Five Elements Society.

And there were tales that inside this imaginary district—this invisible research institute—there were all sorts of super-technology.

Some say that it had an AI controlling all of the world's ethics, military affairs, and economy.

Some say that it preserved the DNA of great men and saints, and as a result of analyzing them, it could create infinite geniuses in some clone factory.

Some say that the silicon synapses used in the Tree Diagram's processing engine could only be produced with the Imaginary Number School District's sci-fi tech, so no one would be able to reactivate it ever again should something go wrong.

Some say that expert "hound dogs" were investigating the Imaginary Number School District from the shadows, but when they got close to its mysteries, they were kidnapped and tortured for information.

Some say that eternal life has been perfected in the Imaginary Number School District and the test subject is Miss Komoe. But that would be a huge infringement on personal rights, no matter how you looked at it...!

Miss Komoe quietly sighed, beer in one hand.

Himegami sat facing her at the tea table. She patted her hands together, declaring:

"All right, time for scary stories."

"Okay, jeez, just get it over with already please! Hurry up!"

"'Kay. Then here's one. The polynuclear aromatic carbonation that comes about from grilling the meat. It's actually a carcinogen."

"W-wait, scary stories that are actually real aren't fit for summer-time at all!"

"There's no point in worrying about it now. You've already eaten so much of it without knowing."

"That's too much! This is all a plan to whittle away my appetite and monopolize all the meat, isn't it, Hime!"

At the mercy of psychological warfare, Miss Komoe heard the sound of her intercom going *ding-dong*.

"Mh, it looks like we have a visitor. It's probably a circular notice, but Hime, please answer the door properly. In the meantime, Teacher will cook the meat by herself and eat it by herself."

Himegami looked at Miss Komoe, who was making a crabby face, then rose without a sound. As she was about to go toward the door, she suddenly turned, saying:

"That can of beer. Aluminum cans contain metallic poison. If you drink a lot of it, poison will accumulate inside your body little by little. One of the reasons the Roman Empire died out. Is supposedly because they used too many metal tools. Hee-hee."

Her appetite now reduced to nothing, Miss Komoe's entire face created an expression that was about to burst into tears.

"And also."

"…There's something else?"

"I'm the one cooking the meat today. You can just sit there and eat it."

Himegami approached the door, then bent down to look through the peephole to see outside. The newspaper solicitors around this area seemed pretty extreme in their methodology, so if worse came to worst, she'd have no recourse but to chain the door, open it a little, then take her magic stick (gas gun) standing in the entrance. She'd shove it through the gap in the door and chase them away with a fully automatic attack. (Warning: Incidentally, as of 1993, its sale has been prohibited by the Diet due to its excessive power. Its nickname was "head crusher.")

But there was no one to be seen out the peephole.

"?"

I wonder if it was someone playing a prank? Just in case, she armed herself with her gas gun and slowly opened the door. As the door opened out, it hit something with a *clonk* and stopped.

Is there a block or something down there? She lowered her gaze.

There was a sister dressed in white, collapsed. Her head was resting on the door. A curled-up calico was happily wagging its tail right next to her.

"Ai...I'm so hungry..."

This homeless, jobless person dying in the streets mumbled *something.* Himegami closed the door.

"Huh? Who was it?" came Miss Komoe's voice.

"No one," replied Himegami in nonchalance. Then, though, rallying the last of her strength, the girl slammed on the door a couple times. It was no use. Himegami tried opening the door once more. The white nun was holding Sphinx out to her, as if to say, "Please, at least take the cat." This was all really pathetic, so in the end she decided to let Index into the apartment.

"T-Touma never came back, so I thought I was gonna starve to death!" the sister in white said, exhausted. She was already sitting at the tea table, a couple of long chopsticks in a balled fist. *She doesn't feel like anything is wrong with going into another person's house and sitting down at their dinner table. Perhaps that's a talent in its own right,* pondered Himegami. The cat, meanwhile, was sitting on Index's knees, looking up at the ceiling, and opening its mouth a little. It looked like a tactic to snatch the food that Index was going to drop.

They had suddenly gotten a guest, but it would take more than that for the twelve-thousand-yen Splendid Yakiniku Set to leave their stomachs unsatisfied. Miss Komoe, caretaker skills at full blast, ended up taking over sole initiative of the hot plate and starting up the *yakiniku.*

"What are supernatural abilities, you ask?"

Miss Komoe responded to Index, using her chopsticks to flip over a piece of meat on the hot plate. Index, suspiciously eyeing the half-cooked meat, nodded slightly and grunted in affirmation.

"Putting it simply, it's a theory of Schrödinger's, but…You're probably not familiar with the story of Schrödinger in the first place, are you?"

Miss Komoe pointed with her chopsticks as if to say, "Eat your carrots, too, not just the meat," but everyone present ignored her.

"Schrö-ding-er?"

"That's right. Mr. Schrödinger is the name of a quantum physics professor. He gave us a story called Schrödinger's cat. It's extremely cruel and heartless for those of us pet lovers, so why don't I arrange it a bit?"

The meat finished cooking, so she wrapped it in vegetables and placed it on Index's dish. Without hesitation, Index separated them and gave only the vegetables to the calico. The calico, however, refused them with a kitty punch.

"Here I have a single box," began Miss Komoe, taking a box of chocolate that was laying on the tatami in her free hand. "Now, what could be in this box? Yes, the little nun over there."

"Mm. There's obviously chocolate in there! Touma has those at his house, too."

"But there is hard candy in this box."

"That was kind of an unfair question…"

"Now, a question, little nun. What could be in this box?"

"You just said it was hard candy!"

"I did, indeed. But we won't know until we open it up. There's always the possibility that Teacher is lying to you."

"…"

"In other words, two possibilities exist for this box right now: the possibility that chocolate is inside, and the possibility that hard candy is inside. Of course, there's only really one of those inside the box, okay? But both of the *possibilities* are in there, all jumbled up."

Miss Komoe jiggled the chocolate box a little.

"When we open it and check the contents, those two possibilities resolve themselves into a single result. The inside of the box is fifty percent chocolate or fifty percent hard candy. By observing it, we can change this into one hundred percent chocolate. That's what I mean."

"Let's check inside," she said, opening up the box. Inside were small chocolates.

"Now then, what if..." She closed the box again. "In this box, there's both a fifty percent possibility to be chocolate and a fifty percent possibility to be hard candy. Now, little nun, what do you think is inside this box?"

"??? I don't really get much of this, but I just saw chocolate in there!"

"That's right. At this point in time, a normal person can only take the fifty percent chocolate possibility. However..." She shook the box a bit. "What if there was someone who could take the fifty percent hard candy possibility? What would happen?"

"Hmm? If that was the case, then the inside of the box would change into hard can—"   •

Index appeared to realize something as she said it.

Yes, something out of the ordinary, something *supernatural*, would occur.

"**That** is indeed the true identity of espers' abilities. Many possibilities exist in our reality. Some of these are fire coming from your hands or reading somebody's mind. This one percent of 'unnatural possibilities' is left out of the rest of the ninety-nine percent of common sense, but it's exactly what *supernatural* abilities are." Miss Komoe twirled her chopsticks around. "On the other hand, that's why these abnormal powers aren't omnipotent. For example, there are only the two possibilities in this box—fifty percent chocolate and fifty percent hard candy—and the chances of bubble gum coming out of it are zero percent. These powers can't be used in places or conditions where something isn't possible in the first place."

"???"

"What we call *espers* are those people whose power to see the reality of this fifty percent chocolate and fifty percent hard candy has been *shifted away* from that of normal people. RSPK Syndrome—in layman's terms, some children lose the ability to perceive reality as it is because of poltergeists, or via trauma or excessive stress. Also, the Gantzfeldt Experiment used in Ability Development purposely shuts down your five senses and essentially cuts you off from normal reality." Miss Komoe spun her chopsticks some more. "An 'esper' who has been cut off from the usual reality can acquire a personal reality that differs from the rest of us. As a result, they alter the microscopic world using different laws than regular people...They can acquire 'powers' like breaking things without touching them or seeing the future a year from now just by closing their eyes."

Miss Komoe's words sounded like they were all from an alien planet, and Index had no clue what she meant.

"The 'Mnemonics' we carry out refers to artificially creating one of these personal realities. To put it more simply, we help cause certain kinds of disorders in their brains by using things like medicine and suggestion."

However, the word *disorder* pierced into Index's chest.

There was a certain boy who always said that he didn't have any power. He would claim this casually, like it was obvious. But there was a lot of hard work piled up behind those words.

It's beyond salvation, thought Index.

She didn't mean the boy who couldn't obtain anything no matter how hard he tried. She meant the boy who smiled and accepted not obtaining anything as the obvious outcome. He was beyond salvation.

"Well, actually, people like Kamijou are the ones who matter."

"...? You know about Touma's power?"

"Well, Kamijou has been a naughty one since he first enrolled, after all. A lot has happened. Yes, a lot. Ehee-hee, ehee-hee.

"Hee-hee," went Miss Komoe, pressing both hands to her cheeks and wiggling around. Index and Himegami saw that and simultaneously stopped moving. In their minds were the words, *Not again! That jerk!*

"Although, Teacher personally believes that it's the Level Zeroes, not just Kami, who present the most opportunity for research." Miss Komoe was the only one who didn't realize the change in the air in the room. "Everyone *should* awaken powers by going through the fixed Curriculum for Ability Development. Despite that, there are people who don't awaken to anything. That means that there has to be some law that we haven't figured out yet. In fact, they may just be the key to figuring out the *System*."

"System?"

"It refers to the one who arrives at heaven's intent in an ungodly body. Our objective is to see what lies beyond Level Five, after all. We humans don't understand the truth of the universe. So it's simple. If there were someone with a status above human, they should obviously be able to understand God's answers."

"…"

Index stopped moving in shock.

She remembered hearing those words. In Kaballah, there is a concept called the Sephirothic Tree. It was a ten-tiered hierarchical diagram describing the ranks of humans, angels, and God in an easy to understand manner. Unfortunately, the all-important God wasn't depicted on it.

Ein Sof Ohr (000), Ein Sof (00), Ein (0).

These, the territories of the gods, cannot be understood by man. Their concepts are inexpressible by human tongues, so they are not displayed on the Sephirothic Tree.

However, a religious system had appeared and flipped this around.

It was a doctrine, which said that if humans are incapable of understanding something, then they needed to obtain bodies above those of men.

Humans are undeveloped gods, and by training oneself, one can attain the body of a god and freely control the works of God—this is what was said by the first maverick heretics of Crossism, who were considered dangerous by even John of the Twelve Apostles.

Gnosticism—the doctrine of a perfect intelligence.

"Ars...Magna," whispered Himegami, touching the giant cross at her chest.

Yes. The man who had once used alchemy to reach Ars Magna, in terms of his lineage, at least, matched this. Because in alchemy, Ars Magna—the "great work"—was not a method of transmuting lead into gold, but rather an art to sublimate a human soul that was dull as lead into the golden soul of an angel.

Those of occult practice, who had strayed from the straight and narrow, were prone to take a liking to Gnosticism. But how had that taken root in Academy City? This place was the polar opposite of the world Index lived in, the Church. Did that imply that people may think differently, but their ultimate destination is the same?

Or perhaps...

The color of the sky had fully shifted into night's deep blue.

...I wonder if Index is all right.

Kamijou recalled the sister in white who was (or should have been) waiting for him back at his student dorm. *It would be a mistake to expect any cooking skills out of Index, so maybe she's stomping around the room in hunger,* he thought.

He considered giving her a call with his cell phone, but he decided against it.

When he called her last week from Misawa Cram School, it had ended up dragging her into a battlefield she shouldn't have gotten wrapped up in.

"..."

Cutting short his thoughts of Index, he turned again to the task at hand.

First, he was heading toward Tokiwadai Middle School's dormitories in search of Mikoto Misaka.

Many of the bus stops in Academy City were named with a school establishment, such as Twelfth School District: Takasaki College Front or Twenty-Second School District: Shizuna High Pool Front. It was natural, what with all the buses in Academy City being school buses.

It turned out that there was simply a bus stop called Seventh School District: Tokiwadai Middle School Dormitory. Normally, the city buses were set up to make their last run at the end of the school day. Apparently, though, on this line, there were provisional buses running at night for cram school summer classes. He expected nothing less of a private institute.

"Here we are."

Kamijou got off the bus, black cat in one hand, and looked up at the building. All around it were the usual concrete buildings, but for some reason, this three-story was the only one built out of stone. It was a very western-looking building that seemed to have an odd history just plopped down here. It almost looked like it was a boardinghouse from a foreign country that had just been disassembled and imported here. There wasn't anything like a courtyard; it was just suddenly *there*, standing beside the road, like a business building.

It was a little bit funny that in spite of the structure being awfully majestic, there were clothes being hung out to dry from windows like you might see normally. The cat, reacting to the things fluttering in the breeze, swayed its head from left to right with the clothes.

He went for the front entrance, but as he expected, there was a strict lock on it. At first glance, they were wooden double doors, but they were likely some sort of special material—carbon fiber, perhaps. In any case, it seemed that the entrance wouldn't sustain a dent even if a truck slammed into it.

Inside the old-fashioned (or at least made to *seem* old-fashioned) keyhole, he saw a red, shining lamp, telling him that there was probably a sensor in the doorknob. *It probably takes your fingerprint and maybe the bioelectricity from your skin or your pulse pattern and investigates them. Or maybe it looks up your DNA code from the fat on your finger,* thought Kamijou noncommittally. .

A ton of mailboxes sat in lines next to the door. It wasn't far removed from the newspaper boxes in apartment buildings. As far as he could tell from looking at the names written on them, Mikoto lived in room 208.

All he had left to do was use the intercom. This was the same as those in apartments as well—it was set up so a person could input the room number using a calculator-like keypad and be put directly through.

Contacting Mikoto's room would be simple. He just had to press the buttons for two, zero, and eight.

Straightforward though it may have been, Kamijou's fingers paused in the air.

Thinking about it logically, there couldn't possibly be any way Mikoto wasn't involved in that "experiment" at all. The somatic cell clones of her, the Sisters, would have needed her to cooperate with the people in the experiment so that they could actually obtain her cells.

What should he say when he saw her?

This experiment was horrifying. It killed people so casually, so Kamijou was scared of hearing the details of it from her mouth. He dreaded seeing her face as she told him the hidden truth.

The black cat meowed restlessly.

Kamijou thought back to the girl he had met at the vending machine. She showed no embarrassment around strangers.

Could that *really* all have been an act to cover the truth?

Or was it some strange, actual intent? Did she *want* to cooperate with the experiment, then go on smiling even though she knew the Sisters were dying?

Neither of those things was the picture that Kamijou had in his head of Mikoto Misaka.

His false image would crumble to pieces as soon as he hit the intercom.

And then, he realized that at some point, he had become frightened of that fake vision breaking apart.

He didn't have a reason.

He probably just thought it had been nice to walk home with her.

"..."

Will you press it anyway? His fingers trembled. If he did, there would be no going back. He wouldn't be able to cancel it. After this, the facts that he was ignorant of would, without a doubt, surge into him like a roller-coaster car starting down a steep hill.

He didn't know what he should do.

Without knowing what to do, his fingers pressed the intercom.

He heard the *click* of plastic buttons being depressed.

Beep, went the speaker, opening a portal to an alien world.

"Ah, umm…"

He didn't know what he should say.

But he needed to say something.

"…This is Kamijou. Is Misaka there?"

The words that escaped his lips were extraordinarily unconventional.

Those mere few seconds of silence, awaiting the voice of the person on the other end, felt frightfully grave to Kamijou. He heard some kind of noise from the other end. It was the sound of someone inhaling. The usual Mikoto was probably across the intercom. Mikoto in the peace of mind that Kamijou knew nothing of any experiments.

The intercom's silence lasted only a short moment.

"Huh? Is that you, Mr. Kamijou?"

He heard the awkwardly slow-moving voice of someone who was definitely *not* Mikoto.

"Ah, oops…Is this the wrong room?"

"Oh no, no, you're absolutely fine. Did you need something from Big Sister? I share a room with her."

I've heard that voice somewhere. Kamijou thought for a moment, then remembered. It was the middle school girl who had called Mikoto "Big Sister" last night—her name was Kuroko Shirai.

"Er, all right. Then I take it Misaka hasn't come back yet?"

"This is the case. But it is my belief that Big Sister shall return quite soon, as the security on the entrance down there is aligned with the curfew." The drawn-out tone of voice continued over the intercom. "If you have something you need from Big Sister, I would recommend coming in and waiting for her. After all, I cannot advise you two missing each other."

The intercom cut off with a *click*, and he heard the sound of the entrance lock being opened. From the multiple *tick-tick-clink* metallic sound, he deduced that the door utilized a number of different locks at once. The cat seemed surprised at the somewhat savage noise.

...Is it really okay...

...to go in like this? he thought, angling his head. But right now, he wanted to hear what Mikoto had to say, so he decided to take her roommate up on her offer.

Passing through the entrance brought him into a giant hall. It certainly seemed like nobles were living here; the keynote color of the walls and ceiling was white, and a red carpet laid on the floor stood out like a sore thumb. At first he thought it was just the vulgar, bad taste of the newly rich, but he got the feeling that this loud color scheme would quickly bring the presence of any intruders into bold relief.

Whether there was soundproofing involved or everyone here was just plain polite, the interior of the building was wrapped in the sort of quiet one would find at a shrine or a temple. Ignoring the passages leading to the right and left from the foyer, he headed toward the stairway in the middle, which led to hallways on the second and third floors. As far as he could tell from the mailbox, Mikoto's room was 208. *Which probably means she's on the second floor,* he thought reasonably.

He ascended the stairs and exited onto the left path on the second story.

He found room 208 almost right away. The room number was indicated with gold lettering on the wooden door, and meanwhile, the cat was having a staring contest with its own face reflected in the polished doorframe. *It's like a hotel room,* he noted. He noticed the absence of an intercom on the room's door as well, also in the same fashion as a hotel.

Kamijou knocked unobtrusively, and a voice answered back from within.

"Come in. The door isn't locked, so please open it up yourself."

Swinging it open revealed what was indeed a very hotel-like room. On entering, Kamijou saw a door to what seemed to be a unit bath standing to the side, and the only furnishings inside were two beds, a side table, and a small refrigerator. There was no notion of a closet. It appeared they kept all their personal possessions packed into the giant suitcase beside their bed.

Kuroko Shirai was still in her pigtails, not having let her hair down even within the room. She was sitting somewhat unnaturally on one of the beds, still clad in her summer uniform.

She didn't pay even a passing glance at the black cat in his hands, as if she didn't have much interest in animals.

But, well...

Kamijou looked the place over again. Despite having received permission from her roommate, he was uncomfortable coming into their room while the one he actually came to see was absent. Kuroko Shirai noticed his look and gave him a small smile.

"I'm sorry. This room is really only for sleeping in, so it's not set up to treat guests properly. If you're waiting for Big Sister, please have a seat on the other bed."

"...Er, I don't think so. I don't have her permission, and—"

"There is no need to worry. That bed is mine."

"What the heck are you doing?! What are you, some kind of pervert, rolling around on someone else's bed like that?!"

"Mgh, I cannot let that one go. Humans all have things they can't tell anyone else, that they think are perfectly okay. Like putting your mouth on the recorder of the girl you like or stealing her bike seat. Things like that."

"No, they don't! How in the hell do you manage to warp such pure feelings like that?! You, Mikoto...You call yourselves proper ladies?!"

In spite of his shout, Kuroko's cheeks puffed out, unconvinced.

Jeez, Mikoto must have a pretty rough time of it at school, too, he reflected, leaning his back against a wall.

"But anyway, I thought you were surely a grade lower than her, since you call her Big Sister and everything. So you were classmates after all."

The black cat began to struggle around, staring underneath the bed, implying it had an interest in narrow, enclosed spaces. He didn't let it out of his arms.

"No, you misunderstand. I am indeed Big Sister's full-fledged underclassman. I just got her previous roommate to go away for a little while...using completely legal methods, of course."

She's scary! Kamijou grimaced a little, and Kuroko mentioned, "...It's because Big Sister has lots of enemies. Though it's the case for someone who possesses such power, don't you think it would be just too harsh for her to share a sleeping space with a traitor?"

"..." He fell silent. The cat stopped fussing and looked up at him.

"In any case." Kuroko looked back at him. "You wouldn't happen to be the gentleman who starts up fights with Big Sister all the time, would you?"

"?"

He didn't really know if what she said was true, since he had no memories. It seemed like he and Mikoto were familiar with each other before, but he couldn't quite pin down what their relationship was like.

Kuroko took a look at his mystified face and heaved a sigh. "... If I'm wrong, then that's okay. I just wanted to have the honor of seeing, if only for a little bit, the face of her support system."

"Support system?"

"Yes. Though Big Sister doesn't realize it yet. My goodness! If somebody always goes on ranting about a person with a gleeful look, whether it's during meals or while bathing or while trying to go to sleep...well, *anyone* would catch on." Kuroko let out a breath. "...Honestly, if Big Sister wanted allies, she doesn't have to look any further than here. When she makes that face, like it's the only place in the world where she belongs…that can definitely get to me a little."

Kuroko started to cower a little, but Kamijou leaned his head to one side.

"…? Is she really that kind of person? I feel like she's at the center of a circle, always using leadership whenever and wherever she is."

"That's exactly why, you know? Big Sister is used to being a leader all the time, so even if she can stand at the middle of the ring, she can't mingle with those outside it. She stands above others, and even though she can defeat enemies, she can't avoid making them…What someone like her needs is a person who will view her as an equal. Well, those are my thoughts on the matter anyway."

"…" Kamijou thought back to Mikoto when they had been together that evening.

She was selfish, quick to answer, didn't listen to him, and if anything bothered her, she'd go all buzzy-buzz on him. But she also seemed to him to be very relaxed. It was as if she was stretching out wide, released from the pressure weighing down on her shoulders during the day.

Walking the road with him after school was probably a safe zone for her.

The smiles she made were honest enough to make him think so and were altogether defenseless.

However…

Was that truly the case? Was the only time she smiled when she was with him? Wasn't there the possibility she was just crazy enough to grin carelessly and always insist on having the last word with Kamijou, even though she watched the Sisters dying before her eyes?

His own thoughts made him want to throw up.

Why can't I trust her? he thought, doubting himself.

"Big Sister probably feels shy about it without realizing—" she said, dreamily looking at a spot she would never reach. "And because she's so embarrassed, she takes on a more, you might say, *aggressive* attitude than necessary."

Kamijou quietly inhaled.

He had thought Mikoto was scary just before. And he was ashamed at himself for thinking that. But he couldn't stop himself from feeling that way. If Kamijou's guess was correct, then Mikoto knew of the experiment, understood that the Sisters were being killed so cruelly, and was *still* cooperating with them.

And even though she was aware of all that, she walked along next to Kamijou with a smile.

It was as if there was a mush of squishy organs on a table with dinner placed atop them, and she was chomping down on the food and loving it—that kind of weird example crossed his mind.

Kamijou didn't want to think she was that sort of person.

He felt hesitation again at asking her of the experiment and hearing it from her own lips.

But that didn't mean he could leave Little Misaka like that.

In the end, he didn't have a clue what he should be doing.

Then...

After thinking all that, his ears picked up the *clip-clap* sound of footsteps approaching from the hallway outside the door. The black cat's ears perked up.

A sticky sweat broke out on his palms.

Mikoto...is she back?!

That's what he was waiting for, but for some reason, a fierce nervousness and anxiety befell him. His heartbeat grew irregular, beating with odd force.

Kuroko, meanwhile, listened for a moment, then leaped out of bed.

"That's bad. There's a residential adviser going around!"

"...Huh?"

She waved her hands around at Kamijou, who was staring blankly at the unexpected perspective.

"Wh-what'll we do? If the RAs see you, it won't be pretty."

"You seem pretty sure it's a residential adviser. How can you tell that by just their footsteps?"

"They're dangerous enough to warrant being able to. Anyhow, they're a pure evil that does surprise inspections on the rooms, so if you could hide yourself under the bed or something, that would be great."

No sooner than the words had left her mouth had she grabbed ahold of Kamijou's head and was trying to force it underneath Mikoto's bed. The black cat cried out in discontent.

"Ow! You know, this is crazy, I can't fit under here! Think about this rationally! *Rationally!*"

"I'm telling you, a gentleman being present in the girls' dorm of Tokiwadai is not normal at all! Damn, what a pain, I'll just use teleport and...huh? Hey, why isn't my power working on you?!"

"Well, I mean, that's probably my right hand...Ow! Hey! Listen to me, you...!"

After a bit of this and that, Kamijou and the black cat ended up stuffed underneath the bed like luggage in a car trunk. To his surprise, it seemed quite clean down here. There wasn't a speck of dust to be found.

...But wait, people wear their shoes in this room! Doesn't that essentially mean, figuratively, that I've currently got my face on bare ground?!

Though the underside of the bed was cramped, there was something else that had arrived there before him: a huge stuffed bear crammed under here. It was about the same height he was.

The place was extremely confined, so as Kamijou was reflexively pushing the stuffed animal around himself, in came the sound of a door opening, no knocking included. He heard a low female voice.

"Shirai. It's time for dinner, so assemble in the cafeteria...Misaka? I have not received an outing notice from her, so you don't mind being docked a point due to shared responsibility if she breaks curfew, right?"

It seemed it was actually an RA.

He was in a relatively desperate situation, but for some reason he felt relieved—at the fact that it wasn't Mikoto Misaka who had entered the room.

This time he heard Kuroko.

"No, no. I think that if it was really something urgent, she wouldn't have had time to turn in a notice. I cannot accept a point dock because I believe in Big Sister."

Kuroko had apparently pushed the RA out of the room and left. Kamijou stayed there for a little while, rigidly. He couldn't see his surroundings from underneath the bed, so it could end up turning into one of those things where the RA would come back in if he nonchalantly crawled out.

Whew...

If things are like this, then getting out of this place is gonna be a pain in the ass, he thought with a sigh. He shot another look at the stuffed bear crammed under the bed with him.

He had considered it a fanciful taste quite unlike Mikoto...but when he looked more carefully, he saw a bandage wrap concealing one eye, and the entire body was covered in more bandages, too. The stitches decorating it brought it from fanciful to funky. The black cat stared unwaveringly at the stuffed animal.

Then all of a sudden it whipped out a punch at its face with its front leg.

Despite his life-and-death situation of being hidden under a bed in a girls' dormitory, Kamijou thought, *That was a cute kitty punch.* Kamijou, who found it heartwarming enough to cause trouble, suddenly heard a brutal *scritch* sound.

"Gah! D-don't start with the clawing, idiot!"

The cat cried out as Kamijou tore it from the stuffed animal and patted the surface of the cloth. That was when the palm of his hand felt something stiff and hard, quite unusual for a stuffed animal. It felt like something was inside.

When he gave it a closer look, a few of the stitches here and there had been modified into zippers. It had a lot of little pockets in it. As he ran his hands over the stuffed animal to see why, he felt what seemed to be a small jar or bottle. Maybe she was hiding perfume in it. Did the cat's nose not take a liking to the smell? It seemed to him that Mikoto was concealing something in there that was against school rules. Like a drug smuggler.

Taking the size of this big stuffed animal into account, she probably had quite a bit of whatever it was she didn't want other people to see in there. Kamijou sighed and removed his hands from the bear...

"Huh?"

Then Kamijou noticed something. There was a thick collar wrapped around the bear's neck like a pants belt. There was "Killerkuma" or something written on it, but that didn't matter.

He tried looking from above and saw a zipper attached in a straight line across its neck, hidden by the collar. It was set up so it would be difficult to open because the tight collar was in the way. In addition to the collar being a decoration, it had a rugged padlock attached to it. This zipper clearly worked differently from the others.

Whatever was hidden inside there was probably the thing Mikoto most wanted to keep away from the eyes of others. Kamijou didn't consider going all the way and seeing what it was. However, the zipper was half open. It looked like there was some paper in there. The corner of a paper was sticking out from inside the semi-opened zipper. That was all. It was all it was. *I should just leave it,* he thought. *Digging around for other people's secrets is bad. It's bad.* But on that paper, this was written in the font of a word processor:

"Trial Number 07-15-2005071112a
Relating to the Sisters, the mass-produced Radio Noise espers, the Level Five One-Way Road 'Accelerator's' "

Kamijou gave a start. The paper was only sticking out of the zipper a little bit, so he couldn't read any more. He shut his eyes. This was probably something he wouldn't be able to come back from once he saw it. So if he didn't look at it, he could still turn back. This was his final warning.

The perfume-hating black cat took a long, menacing breath.

"..."

Kamijou pondered this for a moment, then opened his eyes.

Pretend I didn't see it...? If I was clever enough to do that, then I wouldn't be in this situation in the first place.

In order to get out the sheet of paper, he needed to open the zipper all the way. Unfortunately, the collar with the padlock on it was wrapped around the zipper, covering it up, and presenting him with an obstacle...Well, that's what one would normally think. However, this was a stuffed animal. He squeezed the bear's head as hard as he could. The soft silk floss easily deformed, widening the gap between the bear and its collar. Then he shoved his free hand's fingers into it and opened the zipper.

Close to twenty sheets of report paper came out. It looked like all the data had been printed, but he checked the date and the name written in the corner of the page.

"Utilization of the Sisters, the mass-produced Adepts dubbed 'Radio Noise': Method for the Level Five Superpower 'Accelerator' to evolve to the Level Six Absolute"

That was the name of the report.

Level...Six?

Kamijou leaned his head to one side, puzzled. The current highest level should be Five.

He crawled out from underneath the bed and skimmed over the letters on the report again.

There wasn't a single research institute or person in charge written anywhere on there. It was almost as if it was saying that even if it was leaked, there would be no way to prove anything.

The contents of the report were technical, and there were many words that weren't Japanese. Kamijou fully activated his knowledge and tried to convert the words into ones he could comprehend.

"There are seven Level Fives in Academy City.

"However, as a result of the predictive calculations used by the Tree Diagram, it was verified that only one of them was able to reach the as-yet-unseen Level Six, the Absolute. The other Level Five espers would all either mature in a different direction or else their bodies' balance would be destroyed by increasing the dosage of medicine."

There were various graphs alongside the names of the seven Level Five espers, but he skipped over them.

"The one esper who is able to reach Level Six is called Accelerator, the One-Way Road."

Accelerator.

His face bunched up at the unfamiliar term.

There was what looked like a supplementary explanation in a foreign language, but he couldn't read it, so he decided to keep going.

"Accelerator is, in reality, the strongest Level Five in Academy City. According to the Tree Diagram, by using that element, it was calculated that he would reach Level Six by integrating two hundred fifty years' worth of normal Curricula."

When he read what was written underneath there, his heart leaped into his throat.

It said that there was a summary of methods to have a human body active for 250 years on a separate page as reference materials.

"We set the '250-year method' aside for the moment and searched for another way.

"As a result, the Tree Diagram derived a method different from the normal Curricula. In essence, we could stimulate his growth via the use of his abilities in real combat. There were numerous reports that the firing accuracy of telekinetic abilities, pyrokinetic abilities, etc. would get higher, we used this argument.

"The method was to prepare special battlefields and have combat proceed according to predefined scenarios, thus manipulating the direction of his growth toward real combat."

Kamijou's hands jerked to a halt.

Real combat. He got the distinct feeling that those words and the Sister's corpse lying on the ground were connected somehow.

"The result of the calculations carried out by the Tree Diagram simulator set up 128 battlefields and revealed that by killing Railgun 128 times, Accelerator would shift to Level Six."

He had heard the word *Railgun* before.

You know, you should brag more that you defeated Mikoto Misaka, the Railgun.

Which means that the things written here are referring to her, then? he thought. But he felt calling her a "cooperator of the experiment" was pretty inappropriate.

Kill.

Kamijou's hands shook. His breathing went out of whack and he felt like the floor was spinning. Unconsciously, he leaned himself against a wall.

"However, we cannot, of course, prepare 128 of the same Level Five Railguns. Therefore, we gave our attention to a project we were working on at the same time, the Railgun mass-production project: the Sisters."

His heart was beating strangely. He could feel the warmth from his fingertips being stolen away. The black cat's meowing was rattling his brain like a church bell.

"Of course, the actual Railgun and the mass-produced Sisters have different specs. Even being liberal, they are only as strong as a Level Three Expert."

Something about all this is definitely wrong, his mind protested.

"As a result of the Tree Diagram recalculating using these, it prepared twenty thousand battlefields, discovering that by using twenty thousand of the Sisters, we can achieve the same result as above."

But whatever was wrong, it was being followed, and it was being carried out.

"The twenty thousand battlefields and combat scenarios are described on separate pages."

I wonder, just what is written on those ones? he contemplated.

Twenty thousand ways to die. When, where, how, and in what manner would each and every one of those Sisters branded with code numbers die? It was beyond horrifying. The most nauseating part was not the killing, but rather the fact that even the ones to be killed were acting out their roles according to a script.

…It is impossible for Misaka to raise this cat, admits Misaka. Misaka's living environment is remarkably different from yours, explains Misaka.

What did she feel like when she said that?

When she looked at the black cat, what on earth was she thinking?

When she entrusted it to Kamijou, what did she feel?

"We diverted the original project for this Sisters production method.

"We prepared a fertilized egg from somatic cells extracted from Railgun's hair. By using doses of medication Zid-02, Riz-13, Hel-03, etc., we accelerated their rate of growth."

Standing face-to-face with such a hopeless situation...

And yet she still didn't ask to be saved. What could be going through her mind?

"As a result, we are able to obtain a fourteen-year-old body, the same as Railgun's, in roughly fourteen days. Since they are clone bodies made from somatic cells that were originally degraded, because we altered their growth speed via drugs, there is a high possibility that they have a shorter life span than the original Railgun, but we can presume that it will not cause their specs to drastically change over the course of the experiment."

Was she in despair?

Was she despairing that she could never be saved, no matter what she chose and no matter how she proceeded?

"The real problem isn't the hardware, but the software.

"Fundamental brain information activity like language, movement, and logic are constructed during the first six years of life. However, the time given to the Sisters, with their abnormal growth, is merely 144 hours or less. It would be difficult to have them learn through normal teaching methods.

"Therefore, we decided to install this fundamental information by using Testament, the brainwashing equipment."

Or did she...

Did she believe that her being killed by someone was a normal, everyday occurrence?

She wouldn't despair, nor would she give up. Had she been under the impression that this kind of hell was, in the first place...

...just an ordinary sight?

"We can perform the first 9,802 experiments on-site. However, due to the battlefield requirements for the other 10,198 experiments, we must perform them outside the premises. Relating to the disposal of the corpses, etc., we will limit the battlefields to a single academic district of Academy City, and—"

This is nuts.
Kamijou crushed the report in his fingers.

"This is unbelievable…"
This is the craziest thing I've ever heard, he thought. *They're okay with killing twenty thousand people just to raise one elite esper…You could search the entire world and not find that kind of reasoning.*
He bit down on his teeth.
But despite that, he had in his hands the insane report.
He was staring at a real-life story cruel enough that it would be prohibited, even if it were fiction.
"This is freaking unbelievable, damn it!"
A girl had been created just to be killed.
She was a clump of flesh, created from a nucleus taken out of someone's somatic cells and buried into an unharmed egg cell, then mixed with a bunch of drugs in some test tube.
A girl who looked fourteen had been living locked up in a cold laboratory this whole time, never having been given a name, called instead by her number.
But so what?
Even if Little Misaka was something created just to be killed, and even if she was just created from a nucleus taken out of someone's somatic cells and buried into an egg cell…Even if she was living in a cold laboratory the whole time, never having been given a name, called instead by her number…
Despite all that, she had extended a helping hand of her own volition when Kamijou dropped all those cans of juice.
When she learned that the calico had fleas, she got rid of them for him.

She didn't show it on her face, but somehow, Little Misaka seemed happy when she was with the black cat.

These weren't remarkable or anything. For a normal person, it might seem like it was nothing, not something to particularly think about, something natural done naturally.

But on the other hand...

That meant that Little Misaka was someone who was able to naturally do things you would think are natural—she was a human.

A lab rat...There was no way it was right to call her that.

"...Why...don't you even realize *that*?"

Kamijou gritted his teeth.

The cat's mewing echoed through the room quiet as a graveyard.

From the fact that this report was hidden here and that Little Misaka was a clone created from Mikoto's cells, there was no doubt left that Mikoto was involved in this experiment. A bloody experiment, one wherein twenty thousand people would be killed. He didn't understand what someone who would cooperate with that must feel. He balled his hand tightly into a fist, and—

"Huh?"

Then he realized it.

This report was originally data that had been printed. On the upper left corner of the copy paper were written the name of the data and a date.

That itself wasn't a problem.

The problem was the pair of bar codes inscribed right next to them. They looked like the product codes on the back of books, one atop the other.

"..."

There were many Internet terminals in Academy City, and each one of them had a specific security "rank" attached to it. For example, cell phones were rank D, computers in libraries and personal computers were rank C, the information terminals used by the teachers were rank B, special institute terminals were rank A, and the board's classified terminals were Rank S. It was like that.

Even if connected to the same Internet, a rank D terminal couldn't access rank C information.

This wasn't the ruling class exerting its authority or anything; it was simply that it'd be a problem for the administration if students could access and view final exam answers or physical examination data—that was all.

Wait a second, this bar code is...

Kamijou peered at the bar code in the corner of the report. Right, as far as he knew, the upper one was the terminal ID and the lower one was the data ID. The bar codes looked like things stuck to a box of candy, and underneath the black-and-white stripes, there were numbers lined up.

The upper—the terminal code was 415872-C.

The lower—the data code was 385671-A.

That's odd, he thought.

The terminal rank was C, but the data rank was A. It was an impossible violation of the rules. Besides, if Mikoto obtained this report via the proper routes, she could have just used one of the A-rank terminals in the research facility.

Which meant that she didn't get it via proper routes.

A hacker...or, more accurately, a cracker? Was that what they were called when they just take a peek at the data instead of destroying it? Kamijou didn't know, and it didn't matter. Anyway, the important thing was that Mikoto did not acquire these documents by legitimate means.

In other words, Mikoto might not have been a collaborator in this "experiment."

"..."

He gave the report another look.

After flipping through a few pages, he suddenly felt something with a harder touch to it, different from the others. He took that page out from the bundle to ascertain the strange texture's identity.

It was a map.

The map displayed all the areas in Academy City. It was folded up many times. When he spread it out, he found it was about the size of a bookcase. He hadn't noticed it until now—maybe because it was in the middle of the stack and because the paper it was on was very thin to begin with.

The map was considerably detailed, showing even the positions of alleyways and buildings. And an *X* mark was drawn in a few places with red Magic Marker.

"…?"

Those markings felt somehow ominous, but the map didn't have the names of buildings on it.

Kamijou took out his cell phone. It had a car navigator and a GPS in it. He entered the coordinates of the *X* marks on the map into his phone, which displayed an enlarged map image that actually had the names on it.

Kanasaki University Muscular Dystrophy Research Center

Muscular dystrophy…? he puzzled. Muscular dystrophy was an incurable disease. In simple terms, it was a sickness where you were unable to send signals to your muscles, and since they no longer moved at all, they would steadily atrophy.

But what did an institution researching muscular dystrophy have to do with this report? His head tilted to one side, he looked up the names of the other buildings with the *X* marks on them.

Mizuho Agency Pathological Analysis Institute
Higuchi Pharmaceuticals Seventh Pharmaceutics Research Center

Kamijou wasn't very familiar with the institutions' names themselves, but he recalled something: the news dripping out of the big screen on the blimp. There had been three cases of research establishments related to muscular dystrophy announcing their retirement of operations, one after another, and it had the entire market worrying about a downturn. The black cat meowed uneasily. What had Mikoto said about that news?

——*I really hate that blimp, you know.*

He drew in his breath. The map buried in this report. The *X* marks drawn in red marker on it. The research institutions that were all similar in the fact that they were studying the disease. If you set the report, the experiment, and the map all equal to one another, then it would mean that **they** were probably the "research institutes" carrying out this "experiment." But what did the company retirements mean? And what did those red *X* marks drawn on the map mean?

Dizziness struck him. He had no idea why...but he had abruptly, unexpectedly, come to a single question.

It's already night, so why hasn't Mikoto Misaka come back yet? What could she be doing right now?

It might have been nothing. Maybe she was just lost in a fighting game at an arcade, spewing steam from her head. But something seemed sinister. The research labs going down one after the other... the *X*-shaped scrawls in red marker inscribed as if following them... the fact that there had been three cases of research establishments related to muscular dystrophy announcing their retirement of operations, one after another, and it had the entire market nervous about a downturn...The *X* marks had been drawn on those buildings on the map as if to crush them, not in black or blue, not with a circle or square—marked with, of all things, a red-colored *X*. What did it all mean?

Kamijou had already arrived at the conclusion that this report hadn't been acquired legally.

He had then speculated that Mikoto might not have been a collaborator with the experiment at all.

What if Mikoto had refused to cooperate with the researchers...

…but then she figured out that they were continuing the "experiment" in direct violation of her own will?

In that case, what would the actions she took be?

If they were taken in order to stop the experiment, then…

"I see…"

If they were taken with Little Misaka—no, all the Sisters in mind, then…

"I…I get it…"

He didn't know what Mikoto wanted to do. But at least there was something he could say for sure.

Mikoto Misaka certainly hadn't thought nothing of the experiment.

He didn't know what her reason was for smiling in front of Kamijou while hiding the truth, but…

If Mikoto Misaka had never thought of the experiment as a simple drop in the bucket, then…

Touma Kamijou could probably make himself her ally.

He got the feeling that there wasn't anything going on sticking around here. No, even if that was the most effective option, he couldn't stand for another second waiting intently here.

Kamijou grabbed the black cat by its neck and burst out of the room. He wasn't paying any heed to the fact that someone might see him. In total disregard of any onlookers who may have been present, he ran down the hallway, darted down the stairs, threw open the door at the entrance, and burst out of the building.

9

Reading the report had eaten up a sizable chunk of time, so the sky was already blanketed in the complete nighttime darkness.

Kamijou rushed through the shopping district.

The black cat in his arms was rocking around, and it raised unpleasant cries.

He had no basis for his current actions. He didn't know what

Mikoto was doing, he didn't know where she was, and he didn't know whether or not he should be worried about it. In spite of that, the very ambiguity, the fact that he *didn't* know plunged him deeper into a pit of anxiety. He dashed onward, not understanding anything, as if trying to rid himself of the unease by engrossing himself in some kind of work.

He ran aimlessly, but he *had* to look for her. The contradiction made Kamijou needlessly impatient. For now, he needed to run through the dark clouds to seek out Mikoto.

However, a certain part of him was relieved.

Relieved at this situation, where he was *able* to worry about her again.

He cut across the crowds of people and continued his sprint. A wind generator's propellers were spinning in the distance. *I can't even feel any wind right now*, thought Kamijou, when suddenly he slammed on the brakes.

Its propellers were rotating despite the absence of wind.

Just that one turbine, about a hundred meters away, was slowly gyrating. *That's weird*, he noted…when something hit him like a brick.

The word *turbine* or *generator* really just refers to a motor. Motors have an interesting characteristic: The axle the coil rides on normally spins when provided with electricity, but one can also create electricity by spinning it physically. In addition, a person can get the motor to turn by pouring specific electromagnetic waves into it. That's how the microwave generators on the cutting edge of Academy City tech worked.

The propeller—the motor—was gyrating without any wind. In other words, it was reacting to invisible electromagnetic waves.

…If I just…follow them.

Kamijou shifted the black cat in his arms, then shot off running, slicing left and right through the crowds. The young men and women going about their business watched him as he cut through the flow of people, disturbing it, but he couldn't bother with that. Time was not on his side right now.

He didn't even know whether it was spinning in the first place. The wind generator's propeller had only been swaying very slightly. Despite that, he darted forward, chasing the propeller showing that faint sign of oddness, and turned another corner. Little by little, its movement grew more noticeable. Beyond this spinning propeller was another propeller, turning just a teensy bit faster than the first, and beyond that one was a propeller spinning faster still.

It felt like he was steadily drawing closer to some invisible explosion epicenter.

He ran on...

...to the outskirts of the city, where no lights were, invited by the spinning pinwheels on this windless night.

CHAPTER 3

Railgun

Level5

1

The sky's hue was now the black of a lake on a moonless night.

There was a crescent moon out tonight. The light shining from the sneering mouth was all too weak. Far away from the center of the city, this iron bridge had no streetlights. When combined with the black of the river beneath her eyes, it looked like this spot had sunken into darkness on its own.

Mikoto Misaka, alone, with both her hands on the railing, stared vacantly at the distant town lights.

Pale blue sparks fizzed and cracked around her.

The term *lightning strike* might conjure up terrifyingly painful images, but they were a gentle light for her. She still remembered the evening she was first able to use her power. She buried herself inside her futon and flung small, crackling sparks all night long. They had reminded her of twinkling stars. Back then, she had honestly believed that as she grew older, as she grew *stronger*, she might even be able to create a full sky of stars.

Yes, that was before she grew older.

Now, she thought she wasn't even worth having dreams.

"..."

She squeezed the railing, then loosened her grip again.

The simple action caused her to slightly narrow her eyes and smile.

It was an action natural enough for anyone to do.

However, there were certainly people in the world who could not.

"...Muscular dystrophy, huh...," came the words from her slender lips.

Muscular dystrophy is an incurable disease with no known cause, where one's muscles will slowly start to fail. As not moving your body will cause your muscle strength to wane, the sickness steadily steals all the power in your muscles, until finally you lose even the freedom of your heart and lungs.

Of course, Mikoto didn't have muscular dystrophy.

She also wasn't close to anyone who was suffering from it.

But she could still imagine how difficult it must be to live with.

It's not like the person had done anything wrong, and yet from the moment of their inception, their bodies wouldn't work the way they willed them to. They would look at their ailing bodies, know that there was naught they could do about it, and finally, they would lose their ability to get out of bed. No matter how far out they stretched their arms, hoping for salvation, no one would take them in theirs. Mikoto didn't think a life like that was fair at all.

There was once a researcher who asked her if she wanted to try saving those people.

"By using your one and only power, we may be able to save victims of muscular dystrophy," the man in white said, extending his arm to her for a handshake.

Muscular dystrophy is an illness wherein one's muscles don't move the way one wants.

Signals from one's brain are transmitted to muscles by way of electric signals.

If they had the power to manipulate bioelectric fields, then it could be possible to send signals to the muscles by some means other than through one's normal neural pathways.

They might find it within their power to extend the light of salvation to those whose bodies decay over time, who can do nothing about it, who fall, little by little, into that dark abyss inhabited by anxiety and fear.

"..."

Once upon a time, a small child had believed those words beyond doubt.

She thought that if her power to use lightning was elucidated and they successfully "implanted" it, then she could save a lot of muscular dystrophy victims.

That was how Mikoto Misaka's DNA was officially recorded into the Academy City data banks.

Recently, however, rumors of the military Sisters being created from her genome started to spread through Academy City. It wasn't particularly unusual. She was an honors student at a distinguished Ability Development school, Tokiwadai Middle, and she was one of only seven Level Fives in the city. There was certainly no lack of baseless gossip along those sorts of lines, and so she hadn't believed any of them.

Or perhaps she just didn't *want* to.

Reality, however, had snuck up on her and smashed her dream to pieces with a hammer.

"..."

The weaker copies of her, dubbed Radio Noise, developed by the military—the Sisters had already entered into the production phase, and the current situation was one where they could create limitless amounts of clones with the press of a button.

On top of that, the Sisters weren't even allowed the life of a weapon—the purpose of their lives was to be killed as experimental animals...just like dissected frogs.

"Why......

"...*did it have to turn out this way?*" Mikoto whispered, her lips trembling.

She knew why, of course. It was because a younger Mikoto had recklessly given them her DNA mapping. Had that man in white been lying to her from the start? Or had their research once been healthy but had been altered halfway through? She didn't know anymore.

Once upon a time, a girl wished to help those in need...

...and that very desire was transformed into the slaughter of twenty thousand people.

"..."

That's why she wanted to stop it.

She knew she had to put an end to this lunatic experiment even if it came at the expense of her life.

She didn't think that risking your life was cool. She didn't have a death wish, either. In actuality her body was shivering, the energy in her chilling fingertips was withdrawing, and as if there were too much noise around her, she couldn't think straight.

She wanted to shout out "help me" if she could.

But such a thing was forbidden.

Into the back of her mind floated the face of a certain boy. The young man, who was older than her, possessed some unknown power that enabled him to handle one of the only seven Level Five espers in Academy City quite easily, and yet he had been branded with the stigma of a Level Zero Impotent. Despite such undeserved treatment, he had this strength that allowed him to disregard things as being not important—and that attitude was no front, was no bluff. He never let his immense capacity make him extravagant. He could face down anyone indiscriminately, equally, however weak or powerful the person may be. He was a very strong young man.

Now that she was thinking of it, she and this boy had fought against each other on this very bridge a few weeks ago.

He had played the clown and purposely let those unrelated thugs chase him around in order to distance them from the trigger-happy Mikoto, and then he ran away.

If...

Back then, if she had already realized the full extent of this "experiment" hidden in the underside of the city, if she had cried out to him for help, would he have stood up for her?

She knew he would have.

She felt like he would be able to do what she couldn't.

However, she thought asking for his help for her alone would be the coward's way out.

Close to ten thousand Sisters had already been killed because of her. There were no doubts that the remaining ten thousand were already standing on the precipice of death. She thought it unforgivable to beg for help for her own sake, when she, a beast whose hands were stained with blood, flesh, bone, fat, and organs, shouldered such a grave sin.

"...Help me..."

That's exactly why she couldn't let that voice come out anywhere there were people.

Her scared, hurt, and tattered whisper vanished into the night.

"Help me already..."

A cry, one that would never reach anyone, escaped her mouth, unable to endure it.

And then, she heard the meowing voice of a kitten.

Mikoto looked down. The cat's black fur, unlike the darkness, radiated gentle warmth, and it was sitting at her feet. It looked up at her and gave another mew like an innocent child.

Where on earth did this cat come from? she thought, when...

...she heard the *clack* of a footstep.

"..."

She brought her head up.

With only the light from the needle-thin crescent moon expressing the environment around her, on this iron bridge with no streetlights, on this night bursting with *darkness*...

"...What the heck are you doing here?"

That boy arrived, as if cutting his way through it.

He arrived like a hero, rushing to her side after hearing her shouts swallowed by the dark.

2

Mikoto stood there absentmindedly, isolated, on the nighttime iron bridge.

Kamijou honestly thought his heart might break at his view of her from afar. Her face in profile looked so weak, so frail, and so exhausted, like it could just disappear at any moment. She was usually so gung ho, so the sight of her like this made it all the more painful.

That's why Kamijou hesitated to call out to her.

But not doing so was out of the question.

"...What the heck are you doing here?"

Having heard his voice, Mikoto looked at him.

There was the Mikoto Misaka who was energetic, conceited, and selfish, just like she usually was.

"Hmph. I can do whatever I want, wherever I want. I'm Railgun, a Level Five, you know? If some delinquents want to come up to me just because I'm out late, then let 'em. I don't care. Also, I don't really think *you've* got the right to say anything about it."

Nevertheless, Kamijou felt like he'd seen what was underneath her facade, precisely because she showed him such a perfectly ordinary face.

He couldn't stand to see her like that anymore.

So he said...

"...Stop it."

Just for a moment, her expression blinked away, but in the next it snapped back to normal.

"Stop what exactly? Stupid. This is Mikoto you're talking about. You know, the one who kicks vending machines to get her drink? A little evening walk isn't—"

She tried to respond, though unconvincingly, with that doubtful "ordinary" behavior, but—

"Just stop it, will you? I know all about Little Misaka, and the Sisters, and this 'experiment,' and Accelerator, so let's both cut the crap already."

Kamijou pulled out the sheaf of papers.

It was the insane report printed on twenty or so sheets of copy paper. "————————————————————————
————————————"

In that moment, Mikoto Misaka's everyday act shattered into a million pieces.

She probably didn't realize where the muscles in her face were moving; her cheeks twitched like it had broken.

His heart throbbed with anguish.

Kamijou had probably just destroyed something she had been trying to protect at all costs, even to the extent of completely repressing herself.

He started to move forward in spite of that, but…

"Aah, jeez, why do you do this stuff?" she shot back, cutting him off. "If you've got that report, that means you came into my room without asking, didn't you? And then you went looking inside a stuffed animal…You're more persistent than a sister-in-law, you know that? Man. I guess I'm supposed to be thankful or something that you got so deeply into this to the point where you forget what's going on around you, but you know, that would normally get you executed. Executed!"

Mikoto said all this casually, grinning as always.

That smile looked like it had let go of something, and it made his chest hurt even more.

"So would you mind telling me just one thing?"

Mikoto's voice—bright and fairly forceful. Kamijou reflexively asked, "What?"

"In the end, you saw that and thought I needed to be worried about? Did you think that you couldn't forgive me?"

Her voice was oddly cheerful.

It was as if she knew he had come to denounce her. It was as if she thought that no one in the entire world would actually worry about her. Her voice strangely struck a nerve.

"…Of course I worried about you."

His low, crushing voice caused Mikoto's expression to turn to one of slight surprise.

"Well, I guess someone lying like that is better than no one saying anything at all, no?"

She laughed.

She laughed with eyes that had given up on something, with eyes witnessing a distant dream.

"…It's not a damn lie."

The words found their way out of Kamijou's mouth automatically.

"What…?" Mikoto scowled.

"I said, I'm not fucking lying!" he yelled back. Mikoto's shoulders started trembling more than the black cat was.

For some reason, he just couldn't forgive her for making that face.

So this time, he *did* move forward.

"I apologize for going into your room without permission. I did tell your roommate, but that's no excuse. You can shock me with as much of that buzzy stuff as you want for that. But what are *you* doing? I don't think you got this report by asking permission, either. There was this map buried in there. They all seem like institutes researching sicknesses, but what are those red *X* marks drawn on it? It's almost like…"

He paused after getting that far.

Mikoto looked at him and answered quietly.

"…Like they're kill marks, I presume?"

Her voice was emotionless enough to fill him with terror.

It was transparent, and it could freeze someone solid if they had known her before now.

The black cat at her feet looked up at her anxiously.

"Well, that's what they are. But it's not like I went all Railgun on them or anything like that," she said happily. "A single piece of lab machinery costs millions. I just got in through the Internet and used my power to blow 'em to bits. So the institutes that can't function anymore go under, and their projects get frozen for good…"

Mikoto said all this like she was singing and enjoying herself, but there she stopped abruptly.

"...Well, at least, they were supposed to."

"Supposed...to?"

"Yeah. It's actually pretty easy to shut down one or two research institutions. But some other one ends up picking up the experiment where it left off. However many I squash, however many times I get in their way, the experiment just keeps getting passed on. I guess the prospect of the first-ever Level Six is just too sweet for those important scientists to turn a blind eye to."

Her voice really did sound completely drained.

It was as if it contained an enlightened despair, like she had lived a thousand years and bore witness to all the darkness of the human heart.

"...You know those kids? They all say they're test animals with a straight face," she dropped. "Test animals. You know how rats and marmots and stuff get treated?" she said almost angrily. "I looked it up because it was bothering me, but boy, is it cruel. They cut holes open in their live skulls with a saw without even giving them anesthesia, then drip drugs directly into their brains, all in a search for *data*. They see how many millimeters of the medicine it takes before they start coughing up blood and die in agony. They do this every single day and record their results in, like, picture diaries. When they run out of data, they put together a male and a female in a cage. Then, when the experiment is over, they just dump the leftover mice into an incinerator."

She clenched her teeth, and her throat moved like it was suppressing a gag. "Those kids all know exactly what test animals are. And yet they still call themselves that totally calmly."

Unable to stand it, she bit down on her lip.

Unable to stop it, her lip let flow red blood.

"But we have the report, right? If we hand it in properly to the Anti-Skills, wouldn't the board do something about it? Isn't cloning humans against international law?"

Academy City was certainly doing some crazy things—from its

Curricula involving medications and its independent development of rocket technology—but for all its wiggling through loopholes, it was still aware of the *law*.

The city creating twenty thousand clones of human flesh and blood in order to dissect them was clearly in conflict with international code and shouldn't normally be plausible. If news of it leaked to the outside, factions that viewed the city in a less than positive light would use it as an excuse to sweep in and break everything down.

And yet, Mikoto's face was astounded at what he said.

"From a human point of view the experiment is wrong, but from a scholar's point of view, it's correct. Even if it breaks the law, even if they're shouldering huge risks, and even if their methods stray into the inhumane, it's science that 'needs' to be carried out."

"That's insane! Who would let something that crazy—?"

"Yeah, it's crazy. But don't you think it's strange? This city is constantly under the surveillance of those satellites. It doesn't matter how much you sneak around. It shouldn't be possible to fool the eye in the skies."

This put Kamijou at a loss.

That would mean the general board overseeing Academy City was...

"They're keeping quiet about it. And that includes the city police, the Anti-Skills and Judgment, of course. They're in control of the city's laws, so if we just waltz up with a report in our hands, they could just capture *us* instead," she explained, lowering her gaze to the black cat at her feet...as if trying to fight back her anger.

"...This is wrong," he rumbled.

Rules are placed on people to protect others. Not only were they staying silent about people being killed, they would even go so far as to arrest anyone who tried to save them...It seemed distinctly like they were putting the cart before the horse.

Mikoto grinned a little at him.

It was the exhausted smile of an adult directed at a child who didn't understand anything.

"Yes, it is wrong. Relying on someone else is wrong. This is a problem I created, so it falls to me to take responsibility and rescue those kids."

"..."

He fell quiet.

She twisted her small lips a little and continued.

"When you think about it, it's simple. This experiment is to make Accelerator stronger. So things are simple. If the whole Accelerator part goes away, the experiment will fall apart in midair."

In other words, this is what she wanted to do:

Erase Accelerator from existence by her own power.

She would try to save the remaining ten thousand Sisters, even if her hands were sullied with murder.

But Kamijou said, straight and to the point:

"You're lying."

Mikoto's face turned to one of surprise, and Kamijou pressed further.

"I said it. Yeah, I said it, didn't I? To cut the crap. You can't defeat Accelerator. I mean, if you could have, you'd have gone straight for him. You're the one who blasts me with your buzzy attacks just because you get a little bit angry. You wouldn't have been pressed this far and kept quiet like this."

"..."

"Ruining research institutes, tipping off the general board...I *knew* what you were thinking was roundabout for someone like you. You're the type to brawl it out with anyone you don't like, aren't you? You're not some Goody Two-shoes who would look for evidence and tattle to a teacher." Kamijou paused to breathe. "...Since you didn't do that, it means that you *couldn't*, even if you wanted to. Like, there is such a vast gap between yours and Accelerator's strength that it wouldn't even be a fight in the first place."

And he knew even without that logic, Mikoto couldn't kill Accelerator.

Mikoto Misaka stood up because she couldn't allow any more Sisters to die.

There was no way someone like that would be able to justify killing a human being to stop another from dying.

"That's what I'm saying. You can't solve it by fighting him fair and square, but even if you try to go through the back gate, *they're* better at it. So why didn't you ask someone? If you know you can't do something yourself, then all you have to do is ask for someone's help, right?"

She quieted a little at what he said.

Not even the sound of wind could be heard on this nighttime iron bridge.

In the silence, only the black cat was meowing lovingly.

"...By killing Railgun 128 times, Accelerator can shift to Level Six," she said suddenly into the darkness.

"What?" He wrinkled his brow.

"But they can't prepare 128 Railguns," she sung in loneliness. "So they'll prepare twenty thousand Sisters as weaker copies of Railgun instead.

"So then..." The words slid off her tongue like she was talking about an enjoyable dream.

"What if I didn't have that much value?"

Kamijou sucked in his breath.

"Even if he kills me 128 times, he wouldn't get anywhere near Level Six...What if I could make the scientists think that way?" she said, smiling. "The Tree Diagram actually spit out the result that if Accelerator and Railgun were to fight, even if I put my all in running away, I would die in 185 moves. But what if we could settle things more quickly? What if I lost on the first move, then had no other choice but to fall over onto my ass and crawl away clumsily?"

She smiled as she said all this, as if she was really enjoying it.

"The scientists who saw it would probably think this: The Tree Diagram's predictive calculations are wonderful, but even machines can make mistakes sometimes."

She gave a ragged grin as she said all this.

"…" Kamijou bit back on his teeth.

Bringing down the research institute carrying out this experiment wouldn't do her any good, since it would just be picked back up by some other laboratory. To stop them, she needed to make them think that there was no value, no meaning in the experiment in the first place.

That's why Mikoto was about to go throw a match with Accelerator.

Whether by a bluff or acting, she just needed to force the scientists into a mind-set that the simulation the experiment was based on was incorrect.

Even if that meant sacrificing her own life.

But that was…

"Are you telling me that's going to mean something? Even if you fool the scientists one time, they'll just use the Tree Diagram to recalculate again, and if they get the same result, they'll just start the experiment again!"

Kamijou's loud shout caused the cat to twitch in fright.

But Mikoto's returning voice was soft enough to comfort it again.

"It's all right. That won't happen. See, the Tree Diagram actually got shot down by an attack of unknown origin from the ground about two weeks ago. Though the higher-ups are all keeping it a secret to save face. So they can't do those calculations over again."

He had no memories, and she didn't know the details, so neither would understand…the fact that a single strike from the dragon king controlled by a nun in white had plunged through the atmosphere and cleaved a satellite in two.

"Hah. But it's just so ridiculous. That whole 'according to the predictive calculations~' nonsense they're feeding to everyone right now is just data the Tree Diagram spit out *months* ago, and people are still moving in tune to it."

Kamijou remembered what Mikoto said the other evening.

————*I really hate that blimp.*

————*…Because people are following policies decided on by machines, that's why.*

"But this is my chance. Now that they can't use the Tree Diagram to recalculate anything, those third-rates who've just been gobbling up the answers it spits out won't even be able to analyze which parts were correct and which weren't. So if there was just one mistake in their data, they'd be forced to stop the entire experiment. It's just like a computer program having a weird bug and crashing."

That was all this girl could do.

Even if she put herself on the line and threw away her life trying to defend someone…Even though she would do all that, she couldn't even heroically fight the enemy head-on and defeat him, nor could she bravely downright defend someone.

All she could do was this one thing:

Try and prove to them, with her own life as payment, that an answer that was originally correct had actually been wrong.

"…"

Kamijou clenched his teeth.

It didn't even necessarily equate to success even if she *did* go that far with her bluff. If the scientists caught on to Mikoto's act, it would be over. And there was a chance that even if she did prove that the predictive calculations had been incorrect, they would still foolishly resume the experiment.

However, she still couldn't do anything more than that.

The only thing left was to pray to God that the experiment would stop.

"I get it…," he sighed.

He didn't know what emotions were showing on his face.

"You're trying to die, aren't you?"

"Yes." She nodded.

"You seriously believe that by dying you can save the last ten thousand Sisters, don't you?"

"Yes." She nodded.

Then Mikoto moved her foot just one step forward and came face-to-face with Kamijou again.

"Now that you understand, get out of my way. I'm going to meet Accelerator. I've already stolen the data and learned the locations of the twenty thousand battlefields. Before one of the Sisters starts fighting, I'll cut in and end the fight just like that.

"So get out of my way," she said.

"…" Kamijou gritted his teeth.

It was true that there might not be any other way to stop the experiment and rescue the Sisters. There are problems in the world that can't be solved with a fistfight. Whether it was Imagine Breaker or Railgun, this was all just a logical extension of a kids' pretend battle in the first place. They were all too powerless in the face of "organizations" created by the society of adults.

To stop this experiment…

To stand against this adult society, maybe the only way left that would be granted was for Mikoto to die.

He bit down again.

Little Misaka crossed his mind. She had helped pick up the scattered cans of juice without expecting anything in return, got the fleas off of the calico, and yet she was somehow defenseless and bothered by her body, which cats hated. She hadn't done anything bad and now she would positively be killed, and that made his teeth grind.

"I'm not moving."

Mikoto returned his words with a look of sincere surprise.

"You're not…moving…?"

"Nope," he confirmed, standing in her way.

After seeing her like this and hearing everything—after all that, of *course* he wouldn't move.

But Mikoto was not convinced.

Lips atremble with anger, she laid down her next words with a disbelieving expression.

"What…are you saying? Do you know what you're saying right now? If I don't die, ten thousand Sisters will be killed. Or do you have some other way? You're not really thinking that it's okay if they die because they're just degraded copies…?"

The black cat didn't understand human words. But it certainly quivered at hers.

Of course, Kamijou was well aware.

He didn't consider ten thousand Sisters dying to be acceptable. It also wasn't like he had any other plans up his sleeve. He understood the fact that if Mikoto didn't die, ten thousand Sisters would be killed like lab rats. He tried to understand.

And Mikoto was right. He didn't have a clue what he was saying.

"...I still don't want to."

He didn't have an inkling as to what her circumstances were. But she was trying to throw away her very life to save the Sisters. This wounded girl, who thought of others even more than herself, was a wreck and would be killed, alone, and no one else would know—he didn't want to see the kind of "peace" an act like that would create.

"—"

For a moment, and only a moment, a glimpse of surprise crossed her face, but...

...that expression had already disappeared into anger.

"I see. You're gonna stop me, huh? You think the lives of ten thousand Sisters aren't worth anything, huh?"

Tension ran through the air surrounding them with a *frizzle*.

The black cat at Mikoto's feet flopped down its ears in fright.

"I can't stand seeing those kids be hurt any longer. I was only thinking that I'd defend them with my own hands...If you say you'll stop me, then I'll shoot you down right here. This is my final warning, got it? Get out of the way."

Kamijou silently shook his head.

The edges of Mikoto's lips twisted.

"Hah! You're funny. What, you're gonna stop me by force, then? Fine! I won't hold back, either. I still don't know what kind of power you have, but this time, I've got no intention of losing. So ball your fists like your life depends on it..."

A pale blue spark darted from around Mikoto's shoulders with a *bzzt*.

"...because if you don't, you're really gonna die."

The spark that came out of her illuminated the bridge, linked to the handrail, then dispersed. The cat removed itself from Mikoto's side, surprised at the brutal tone this created.

There were just seven meters between the two of them.

It wasn't close enough for Kamijou to be able to cross it in one step, and it was definitely well within range for Mikoto to launch a light-speed lightning attack at him.

It was obvious at a glance which of them was at an advantage and which at a disadvantage.

Words would probably no longer reach this girl.

Now that they wouldn't, there was only one way left to stop her.

"..."

Kamijou thrust his right hand to the side.

He opened his clenched fist once; the action was like he was unlocking a seal on his hand. Mikoto's eyes narrowed slightly. He gritted his teeth so hard his jaw might break, took his opened hand, and...

...didn't close it again.

"Wait, what the heck are you...," Mikoto stammered at Kamijou, who wouldn't move no matter how long she waited.

He didn't reply.

She became indignant, disallowing of his attitude.

"I just told you to fight, didn't I? If you want to stop me, then do it by force! Are you stupid or something? I'm obviously gonna shoot you even if you're defenseless!"

The words full of contempt flew from her mouth like cannonballs.

In response, he answered with just three words.

"......ight."

"—? What did you—"

She lowered her eyebrows just a bit.

"I won't fight."

His words petrified her.

She stared at him like he had three heads.

"Are you...stupid? Hah, you really are a moron, aren't you! I don't have any other way of doing this, so I could easily shoot you in the back even though I trust you, and yet you're saying that! What kind of half-assed world are you drowning in? This isn't your everyday life here, you know! More than ten thousand people have been killed just like that already. This isn't everyday life; it's hell tinted with blood and flesh and fat and organs, and some wait-and-see attitude like that won't—"

"—I still will not fight you...!"

Mikoto's abuse sounded as if the jaws of hells had opened upon him, but even that was erased by Kamijou's roar.

He brought his remaining left hand up and out to the side to form a pair with his already raised right hand. They formed a cross to block her way and as an indication that he had no intent to fight.

"Da...mn. I'm telling you, fight me..."

Her shoulders shivered.

The sparks electrifying her body could no longer be held within it, and all the surplus bluish-white electrical snakes burst out onto the railings and the ground near her, one after another.

But Kamijou still didn't close his fist.

He didn't want to.

The reason he stood before her was because he was worried about her. She was about to set foot into a place dangerous to enter alone, so he wanted to stop her. This wreck of a girl never asked for saving, even until the very end of the end. He didn't want to see her wishing for her own death all alone, and he didn't want her to bear even one more wound; that's why he had wanted to stand here.

And yet he couldn't point his fists at her.

Kamijou could not punch Mikoto.

Looking at him, she spread pale blue flashes from her entire body.

"...I'm telling you to fight me, damn it——!!"

A moment later, she finally shot a spear of lightning from her bangs.

The maximum voltage of a lightning strike born of nature is one billion volts.

Hers rivaled that.

A blue-and-white lance of light created from a ferocious, billion-volt charge. The attack pierced through the atmosphere, broke down the oxygen atoms in the air and rearranged them into ozone, and flew at Kamijou across the seven-meter gap separating them in the blink of an eye.

Whump! came a howling noise.

The blue, electric javelin plunged straight past Kamijou's face.

"I'm shooting for real next time," she said through closed teeth. "If you've got the will to fight, then clench your fist! If you don't, then don't stand in my way! Don't trample all over someone's hopes with your half-assed feelings!"

Crackle, came a fierce cry as sparks burst out of her hair again.

This time, the strike fired straight at Touma Kamijou's heart.

Her attack had her demand behind it: that he clench his fist right now.

Kamijou, despite that, did not.

He didn't want to raise a finger against this girl.

Then the brutally shrieking lightning lance struck him directly in the heart.

3

Feeling like he'd been swept off his feet by a cannonball, Kamijou's body slammed into the ground. He rolled across it like that for one or two meters. His form collapsed with his limbs sprawled out violently, kind of reminiscent of a broken puppet.

"Eh?"

For the first time, Mikoto was more surprised than Kamijou at what she was seeing.

She didn't understand what his power was like, but he had never allowed a single attack to hit him in all the fights they had until now.

Every time he used that strange ability to wipe out her strikes, she rapidly escalated them. At some point, she had begun to see him as an invincible existence, able to easily handle any attack she could throw at him.

That's why she fired the lightning lance.

In some distorted way, she had trusted him...

...to comfortably nullify an offensive of *this* level.

"But..."

...*This has...gotta be some kind of mistake,* she thought.

She looked at the boy lying on the bridge. Mikoto was well aware of what happened to a human body if you poured a billion volts of high-tension electricity into it all at once. That boy would never be standing up again. She knew that. She had done all of this. She knew that. She understood it, but...

Just then, the boy who never should have risen again moved.

He gritted his teeth, rallied all his strength, and stood up.

"Wh..."

She certainly whispered, "Why," then.

Kamijou's power hadn't erased her electricity. It definitely struck his body. And in spite of all that, he had gotten up under his own strength—without relying on any special abilities.

And...

Even after taking a billion-volt surge to the chest, he didn't ball his hands into fists.

That's why Mikoto had dazedly asked, "Why?"

"...I don't...know," he said through clenched teeth. "I don't know why I don't want to fight you. I don't even know if I have some other good plan! But I can't stand it! I don't want to see you gettin' yourself hurt! I don't even know what I'm saying right now! But can you blame me? Of course I don't want to point my fists at you!"

Wha...? She was at a total loss.

The boy was shouting like he was about to cough up blood. He looked ready to collapse at any moment, the way he was desperately planting his feet on the ground like that.

"I don't know what else to do, I don't know what else you should do, but I still don't want to! Why do you have to go and die?! Why do you have to get killed by someone?! Of fucking *course* I can't accept that!"

The boy probably realized that his words were no longer reaching her.

But he still cried out.

He very likely didn't have a reason.

It was just that there was something there—something that made him unwilling to give up despite his logical understanding of it.

"..."

That moment, only for a moment, Mikoto bit her lip.

Once before, there was a girl who had whispered, "Help me," so that no one else could hear.

That boy had appeared, as if to answer her plea.

If she said, "Help me," the boy would doubtlessly bring about whatever miracle they needed.

Mikoto Misaka, though, said to herself that she couldn't allow that to happen.

It was her own fault that more than ten thousand Sisters had been killed.

And yet it would be absolutely unforgivable for her to seek out someone else to fulfill her selfish desire for delivery.

"Shut...up, already," she said through quivering lips. "I don't have the right to get you to listen to my words at this point. Even if there were some perfect world, where everyone smiled and everyone was saved...I don't have any place in it!

"Out of the way!" she roared.

Sparks fluttered from her bangs with a *crackle*.

This time for sure, she thought, he would either have to raise his fist against her or yield the way.

And yet the boy just wouldn't grasp his fists.

The lightning lance, no longer under her control, pierced straight through his chest.

Whump! came a deafening noise.

But the boy didn't die. In fact, he didn't even fall down. He was putting all his strength into his legs, though they were about to give out, and stood there broken but still in her way.

"...You...realize it, too, right? No one is gonna...be helped by this. Even if you die and you saved the lives of ten thousand Sisters...You think they'll be thankful they were saved by you doing this? The Sisters you wanted to save aren't that petty!"

"Shut up! Just be quiet already and fight! I'm not the good person you think I am! I dumped a billion volts of lightning into you, so why the hell do you still not get it?!"

Mikoto fired another spear as if to intimidate him.

But he still didn't put strength into his right hand. The lance of lightning went straight for him, then collided directly with his chest.

And he still didn't go down.

However many attacks he took, he wouldn't go down.

"I already killed more than ten thousand people! There's no reason it would be okay for a villain like me to live in this world! Why the hell are you standing up for a villain?!"

"You're not a damn villain," he said.

Mikoto frowned, doubtful, but...

"If you were a bad person, then why am I still alive?"

"Eh?" Mikoto stammered.

"You said a billion volts. There's no way a normal human could live after being jolted by that kind of high tension. Didn't you think you were doing something strange? Or maybe you were holding back unconsciously or something like that."

"Holding...back?" she said, her face puzzled. "There's...no way. I was ready to kill you. I knew that you were...defenseless...and I knew you wouldn't resist...but I still...!"

"But you still couldn't kill me."

"..." Mikoto abruptly fell silent.

He was right. Normally, a human shouldn't be able to live through being struck by a billion volts.

However, there were exceptions.

For example, store-brand stun guns would deliver two hundred or three hundred thousand volts, but people don't die from that. On the other hand, people can be electrocuted from wall outlets with only one hundred volts and be killed by it.

The reason for this isn't because of the voltage, or tension—it's due to the level of amperage, or electric current. Wattage equals volts times amps, so it doesn't matter how high the voltage is. If the amperage is low enough, you wouldn't die.

In other words, although the voltage of the lightning lance Mikoto fired was terrifyingly high, the amperage was horrifyingly low.

It was just like those fake swords used in period dramas; the attacks they make are for show, without any malice behind them.

But Mikoto didn't intend to go easy on him. She had definitely shot him with everything she had. So she just stood there, looking at Kamijou, not understanding why this phenomenon had occurred.

Fizzle. Kamijou stared at Mikoto, trembling like a scared feline, dead center.

"For you, giving your life to save the Sisters might be your final dream—" he said, battered. "But in the end, despite that...You're a good enough person that you can't even kill the guy trying to steal your final hope, aren't you?" he said, absolutely exhausted, but somehow managing a cheerful grin.

She grunted and faltered, looking at Kamijou confusedly.

Her eyes wavered like a small child who had lost her way.

Mikoto Misaka didn't want Touma Kamijou getting any further into this experiment.

That's exactly why she so easily spoke of all the brutal details when he asked about it. She wanted him to feel hopeless after hearing it. When she one-sidedly attacked him with lightning, it was also because she wanted him to realize he wasn't getting through to her and that he should give up.

If Kamijou had just lost faith in Mikoto...

...then he wouldn't follow her and get involved with this experiment of swirling death.

"Just...stop it."

Her hands grabbed her head.

But he said he would still stop her despite that. However many filthy insults she flung at him, even if she kept on attacking him while he was defenseless, he had declared that he didn't care.

At this rate, that boy would go too far.

He would delve too deeply into an abnormal world far removed from his everyday life—a whirlpool of blood and dirt from which he wouldn't be able to turn back.

"I have to die to save those kids! There's no other way! Isn't that enough?! I'll die by myself, and if that can rescue everyone, that's a wonderful thing, right?! If you think that, then get out of my way!"

Mikoto covered her ears with her hands and shut her eyes tightly.

—But she thought she heard the words *I'm not moving* manage to slip through.

"...You'll die," she muttered, eyes closed. "From here on, you won't be saved! If you take the full brunt of my next attack, you definitely won't survive! So if you don't want to die, then get out of my way!"

The voices of purple sparks flowing around her alternated, heavily and sharply.

The volume got rapidly louder, as if she had activated some strange weapon.

"..."

And yet the boy didn't take one step...

...as if to assert that an attack like this didn't even give him a reason to back off.

Mikoto bit down on her lip.

Bluffing wouldn't work against him.

As long as she wasn't shooting life-or-death strikes at him, she'd never be able to get him to give up.

If he knew this wasn't a bluff, even he should need to fight.

—But still, she was sure she heard his cry that he wouldn't move.

Finally able to endure it no longer, she shouted.

A flash, like piercing her toughly shut eyelids. A roar, like plunging past the hands covering her ears. It wasn't one of weak current and high decorative tension. What she unleashed was a bona fide spear of lightning that could even pierce the heavens.

In a flash, without light or sound…

Wham!! The sound of a direct hit, like a fireworks factory had exploded, rang out.

Despite that, the boy never clenched his right hand.

In the end, the story was as simple as that.

4

Mikoto opened her eyes timorously, and she saw him, lying there a few meters away from her.

He was prone, unmoving. A thin smoke, like the kind produced by joss sticks, was slowly wafting from a few spots on his clothing. In the same way that game consoles heat up when you play video games for a long period of time, a body will get hotter when electricity is passed through it via a process called Joule heating.

It looked like the massive Joule heat created by the high-tension electrical current had charred his body with light sunburns here and there.

However, he no longer writhed from the pain of those scorch marks.

"Ah…"

There, Mikoto suddenly realized it had ended.

This time for sure. This time, unquestionably, that boy would never get up again. The shock had likely stopped his heart, since it was flooded with an *actual* high-tension current rather than a counterfeit one.

She heard the black cat give a meow.

Her body and thoughts both wobbly, she looked back. There, a couple meters away from her, a black cat was sitting scared to death.

It wasn't bristling its fur, though, nor was it baring its teeth or claws.

Those innocent eyes seemed to be pleading with her: Why would you do something like that?

"Ahh..."

When she looked at the cat, she swiftly comprehended.

In the end, Mikoto had done...*that*...to him. It was as if she had suddenly sent a surge of lightning into an innocent, cute kitten nuzzling its nose against her, trusting her with everything it had.

The boy truly did have many options to choose from.

For example, after reading the report, he could have pretended he hadn't and gone back to a false ordinary life.

Even if he had wanted to stop her, he could have concealed the fact that he had read it. Then, when she turned her back to him without having any misgivings, he could have whacked her upside the head as hard as he could and knocked her out.

But he didn't do those things.

He went into her room by himself, directly revealed to her that he had read the report, exposed his true feelings that he didn't want to fight her, made clear all of his own intentions, and still tried to stop her face-to-face.

It was just like playing poker with his hand faceup.

It was akin to declaring he'd shoot scissors before a game of rock-paper-scissors.

Why would he do something that dangerous?

If he had betrayed her trust and assaulted her from behind, he could have ended things much more safely.

"..."

The reason was obvious.

Mikoto trusted that boy. At the very least, being around him presented her with a kind of safe zone, since he didn't know anything about the experiment.

Just like a kitten curled up in the sunlight, taking an afternoon catnap.

It was likely that he *couldn't* have stabbed her in the back. He clearly never wanted to do that, even if it was the safest, most certain option.

* * *

His wish—never to hurt her, even when she held a gun to his head.

His belief—that they could work things out by talking, without resorting to violence.

But in the end, his words didn't reach her, and she pulled the trigger.

"..."

Mikoto gritted her teeth.

There was nothing left to stop her. She felt like she'd been liberated as something like resignation cleanly cut through a slender thread inside her. The sensation was like that of a balloon with its string cut off, free to fly as far away as it could—like she had obtained her freedom, in which some decisive destruction awaited her—

Kamijou's fingers twitched.

"?!"

She was benumbed at the sight of the unbelievable reality.

The fallen boy's right hand, sprawled out to his side, jerked. Those fingers moved slowly across the ground, stroking it gently.

It wasn't in revenge against the person who'd done this to him.

It also wasn't in terror, in a desire to run away as fast as he could.

He had said so from the beginning.

I won't fight. I don't want to fight.

His persistence indicated his want to extend a hand of salvation to a lonely, isolated girl who had cried out for help. That was all.

"...Wh...hy?" she murmured.

It wasn't like he knew everything about her situation just from having read the report. The fact that she had provided her DNA map for the purpose of healing muscular dystrophy, the fact that it had been converted for military purposes before she knew it, the fact that her aspiration to save people had flipped into bringing twenty thousand people to their deaths...

He shouldn't have known any of that.

And yet he had still stood up to her.

He'd stood up…for her.

But that was…

"St…op," she said, a child on the verge of tears, wagging her head to and fro.

If he got to his feet again, she'd have to eliminate him in order to save the Sisters—he was an obstacle. She could go easy on him, of course. But the fact that he was still moving was strange. Even the slightest attack, made for the most playful of reasons, could be the shock that stopped his heart.

So she said simply…

"Stop…it…"

She didn't want him to get up anymore. If he was still alive, she wanted him to just fall unconscious. That way she could go to Accelerator without having to kill him.

If he would just give up on her, no one else would get hurt.

If he would just lose faith in her, he would be released from this suffering.

But he moved his fingers.

Even though he couldn't even move his body. He channeled every bit of strength, every fiber of his being, into his hand, and at the very end managed to wiggle one finger.

"Ahh…"

Mikoto slowly raised her hand toward him.

This boy would probably never stop. Even if his limbs were cut off. Even if his eyes and ears were destroyed. He'd never give up as long as his heart was still beating. So there was no other way. If he was going to impede her saving the Sisters, then she had to get rid of him in order to go forward.

She carefully aimed her palm at him…

…But she could fire no spear of lightning at him.

Mikoto's frozen lacrimal glands took on heat.

It was no use. She couldn't shoot him. She didn't know why. She didn't know the correct answer. She just didn't want to. She couldn't bear to see him die. Just the thought of it made her want to throw a fit.

Help me.

Those two words that she shouldn't have ever let anyone hear came out of her mouth…

…as if she was praying to a god she didn't know existed or not.

Transparent rust fell from the lacrimal glands that should have long ago corroded.

5

Kamijou's vision faded in and out.

He could see Mikoto standing there dumbfounded as he laid there, stretched out on the bridge.

The lightning attacks had stopped.

Tears fell in big droplets from the eyes of Mikoto, who was unmoving, like a small child.

Think…

In desperation, he braced his heart, which felt liable to shatter to pieces at any moment, and considered it absently.

The girl before him had said this: *There's no choice but for me to die*. She didn't say that she wanted to die or that it was okay if she died. She definitely said that **there was no choice** but for her to die.

That was the only important part.

She wasn't wishing for death. It was just that she had no other options from which to choose.

For example, if a person is given three options, then told they absolutely need to choose one of them, but all three of them said "suicide," they can't choose anything except "suicide." It was absolutely wrong to force the kind of responsibility to make that choice onto her.

So think…

If three choices were "suicide," then he just had to get a fourth option ready for her. If there was an option that said "live nonethe-less," then the girl who **had no choice but to** die would definitely choose the new option.

Think of what that fourth option is…

A choice in which the experiment would come to an end with-out Mikoto Misaka having to die. A choice in which not a single person lost anything. A choice in which they could save the Sisters. A dreamlike choice. She had said it herself. She didn't put it into words, but she was definitely saying this:

I actually want to live, but there's no other path aside from me choosing to die, she said.

If you search and can't find one, then make one yourself…

Accelerator would be able to shift to Level Six by killing Railgun 128 times.

One hundred twenty eight Railguns couldn't be prepared.

So instead, they readied degraded copies of Railgun, the Sisters.

The same result could be achieved by killing twenty thousand of the Sisters.

The experiment had been mapped out by the Tree Diagram's pre-dictive calculations.

As soon as she runs a research institute into the ground, the experiment gets inherited by another one.

In order to stop the experiment, they needed to force them to think that the experiment wouldn't be of any value in the first place.

Wait…?

Then Kamijou caught onto something that seemed a little off.

But in the next moment, the repeated exposure to all those high-tension electric shocks caused his faint consciousness to flee hastily into darkness.

CHAPTER 4

Accelerator

Level5(Extend)

1

The chill around her steadily sharpened as night crept into the air. Despite it being the middle of summer, she felt as if a frozen blade were being held against her face.

With a precise, machinelike cadence, serial number 10032, "Little Misaka," passed through the shopping district and into a section of the city containing a quiet industrial area.

Walking through an uninhabited road dotted with a line of streetlights, she ruminated on the details of the experiment about to take place here.

The absolute coordinates of the test location were X-228561, Y-568714. The starting time would be 8:30 PM JST on the dot. The sample to be used was number 10032. Her purpose was to induce an approach during a battle in which "reflection" cannot be applied.

"..."

Little Misaka's mind was saturated with careful considerations of the scenario that would kill her, but her expression wasn't grim. She possessed neither fear nor hatred, nor did the concept of quitting even come to mind.

Her face was simply a true lack of emotion.

Seeing her would likely make a person think of the sense of peril accompanying a clockwork puppet teetering toward the edge of a cliff.

Little Misaka was not, however, a deviant who didn't give any weight to the lives of living beings. Should she be presented with somebody on the verge of death, she had the ability to immediately look up the options she could take and then choose the most pertinent one.

However, she could not direct this toward herself.

Her body could be automatically produced at the press of a button, thousands of times over as long as the requisite materials were procured. Her mind was a void into which information had been installed using Testament, much like overwriting data on a hard drive. One hundred eighty thousand yen was the price tag on Little Misaka's life. She was no more than a high-end personal computer. Even so, if manufacturing technologies sufficiently advanced, she could be sold for a lower price on a large scale—enough that she would be tossed into a bargain sale bin.

…And that is why there is one thing I don't understand, thinks Misaka.

Something suddenly came to her as she trekked down the dark night path.

The boy the many Misakas had encountered in the alley had caught his breath in surprise. It was as if some unbearable fact had been shoved down his throat, and that even afterward, he was saying that he didn't want to accept it.

Little Misaka thought back to what he had said.

————*Who are you?*

Those words weren't meant to question Little Misaka.

————*What are you doing?*

He seemed like he was asking her something so that he could hear her somehow deny it.

Can he really not accept it? she thought, face still impassive.

Can he really not accept this world of twenty thousand Sisters, whose hearts all stop in accordance with their operation?

…I do not know. I cannot understand it, ponders Misaka, harboring doubts as to the boy's state of mind.

I shouldn't think about what I cannot understand in the first place, she concluded, as if to say that it's okay to not know the feelings of a toad swimming in a gutter.

However, if that was the case…

Then why on earth did she recall his face?

If doing so really had no value, then she wouldn't have recalled it at all. After all, there's no need to commit to memory the shapes and colors of pieces of chewing gum stuck to the ground on a train platform a week ago, after all.

She should have been mentally assembling the information regarding the experiment soon to be carried out. If she failed in this situation, she would cause inconvenience for many. Just why did her thoughts digress and bring up the face of a boy with no relation to the experiment?

"…"

Little Misaka couldn't figure it out.

I shouldn't think about what doesn't matter in the first place, she concluded.

She couldn't even understand such a pointless, tiny thing.

Ignorant of it all, she headed alone for her own place of execution.

Her precise footfalls were like a ticking time bomb.

2

Kamijou was lying sideways on the windless iron bridge.

He slowly opened his eyes. The amount of time that had passed while he was unconscious from taking the brunt of the high-tension current was likely short. A digital clock would probably show ten or twenty seconds at the most. However, the tips of his outstretched fingers and toes felt abnormally icy. His normal blood flow was being obstructed. His heartbeat might have grown irregular from the impact of the electric shock, and in the worst case, his heart may have altogether stopped once or twice while he was out.

With hands and feet strewn like a puppet thrown in the corner of a room, its owner bored with it, he stared lazily, without moving his neck.

"..."

He channeled strength into his fingertips to test them, and his index finger moved slowly, like an insect at death's doorstep. He managed to move his eyelids and blink, too. Air was being sucked in and out through the gap between his lips, extremely thin though it was, and he could barely hear his pulse in his sprawled body.

That's a relief, he mouthed.

My body...can still move. That means I can still get back up.

"What...are you doing, idiot?"

He heard a girl's voice above him, extremely nearby.

At last, Kamijou noticed the odd softness pressing against his cheek. It appeared that Mikoto had him resting on her lap.

"...You're so beat up, and you were lying on the dirty ground, and even if it was just for a short time, your heart might have stopped, but you..."

Her voice was trembling.

It wasn't the voice of one of the only seven Level Fives in Academy City, nor did it belong to the young lady of Tokiwadai Middle School called Railgun. It was the voice of a completely ordinary girl, shivering alone in the darkness.

"...How can you still be smiling?"

Clear tears dripped onto Kamijou's cheek from above.

"..."

Thank goodness. He moved his lips, but no voice came out.

Thank goodness I could be her ally. He narrowed his eyes ever so slightly in joy.

The black cat let out a meow at his ear.

A rough-feeling, small tongue was touching his hand, as if it was gently licking his wounds.

"I've got it," he said, still limp. Mikoto didn't answer. The only sound that reached him was that of her rubbing her eyes with her fingers to dry her tears.

"...I figured out a way to stop the experiment."

Mikoto's throat made a *hic* noise as she caught her breath in surprise.

"It's so simple I wonder why I didn't think of it before."

This entire experiment was just a bunch of scientists following a scenario described by the Tree Diagram. That's why Mikoto had thought that if she could make them think this "scenario," which was actually correct, was wrong, then maybe the experiment would stop.

Yes—if that was all it took to stop the experiment, then the rest was simple.

"...I mean, the fact that Accelerator is the strongest in Academy City is obviously part of the Tree Diagram's calculations..."

If they could stop the experiment just by leading them to believe a bluff, then...

"...Then it's easy. They keep going on and on about how Accelerator is the strongest, so we just have to make the scientists think like this: He is actually really weak."

Yes—for example, if Accelerator, spoken of as Academy City's toughest...

...What if he got beaten easily in some pointless road brawl?

Even if the simulation's results described him as strongest in the city, would they still go on thinking that way after seeing him lose pathetically?

Wouldn't it be possible...

...to make the researchers think that the prediction given by the machine was mistaken?

"That's impossible...," Mikoto answered shortly. "The experiment won't be stopped with such a simple method. I mean, I'm Level Five, same as him, right? If Railgun defeats Accelerator, the same rank, the scientists would probably think it was within their margin of error. They wouldn't think Accelerator was actually weak or anything," she muttered, frustrated...

...like she was clenching her teeth, like she was stained with blood.

"And besides, even if we teamed up, we still couldn't beat him," she said, biting back anger at her own inability. "I've only ever seen Accelerator directly once. But I could tell from just that. All I did was look up his ability a little in the data banks, and I got goose bumps from it. The way he fights doesn't involve winning or losing. For him, fighting means one-sidedly murdering his opponent."

"..."

That's probably true, noted Kamijou.

The Tree Diagram had already derived that if Railgun and Accelerator were to fight, the odds of Mikoto coming out alive were 185 to 1. This was probably an exceedingly *correct* answer. Even if Mikoto Misaka tried every means available to her, however hard she tried, she would never be able to defeat Accelerator. That's why the impulsive, straightforward Mikoto also couldn't just go up and punch him and, in the end, got herself to thinking that the only way to stop the experiment and save the Sisters in the end was for her to be killed.

Kamijou understood. It was easy to see that Mikoto Misaka couldn't beat Accelerator.

"Then it just has to be *me* fighting him, right?"

Mikoto swallowed her breath in astonishment at that.

But there was no other way.

If a Level Five defeated a Level Five, they couldn't get the scientists to think that Accelerator was really a weakling.

If, however, Touma Kamijou, the weakest Level Zero in Academy City, were to beat up Accelerator, the strongest Level Five in Academy City...then what?

Of course, they could end up thinking he was actually a ridiculously strong esper, despite being someone who had low marks up until now. However, the city's System Scan had pried into all the nooks and crannies of his body; he would never be able to remove the stigma, the letter, of a Level Zero Impotent, because that's just what his Imagine Breaker was.

Accelerator, losing cleanly to Kamijou, a Level Zero by all measurements.

Would they really think he was the strongest in Academy City after that?

"..."

Now that he knew what to do, the rest was simple.

Kamijou tried to lift his head off of Mikoto's lap, but his body wouldn't move properly. A stabbing sensation shot through him as his head slid off of her onto the hard ground beneath.

But he could still grit his teeth and move his fingers, quivering like caterpillars. Slowly, slowly, his five fingers caught on a groove in the asphalt. Then, mustering all the strength in his body like he was lifting a barbell, he finally brought his body off of the ground.

Kamijou's body felt so exhausted as he knelt there on one leg that he thought five years had shaved off his life span.

Seeing him holding it in like that, Mikoto asked, her voice shaky...

"What...are you doing?" as if she were witnessing something she couldn't believe. "There's no use. You're only saying that because you don't know Accelerator's ability! I'm telling you, it's ridiculous to think you can fight some rule-breaking manga villain...some guy who can turn all the armies in the world against him and grin and take them head-on!"

"..." He didn't respond.

He simply, silently, pushed more strength into his feet to try and stand up further from his current kneeling position.

"Accelerator's real ability is that he can freely manipulate the vector of anything, whether it's momentum, heat, or electrical current, just by touching it with his skin. Even though we know his power, we can't find a way to beat him! It's totally unfair!" Mikoto shouted, as if at the all-too-outrageous reality itself. "All of his attacks hit you, but none of yours hit him, since just by shooting something it'll get reflected. There isn't a human alive who can stand against that absurd One-Way Road!"

"..." He didn't respond.

He poured all the power he had into his shaking knees in an attempt to stand, still trembling rigidly.

"He's something else! Think of him as some kind of other-dimensional being as the rest of us espers. From the start, there's no way you can win by facing such a rule-breaking human from the front. And not to mention your body right now! Like that...against a monster like him...

"...You can't possibly win," she whimpered in a voice that sounded like she would cry. "Please don't stand up again," she begged him.

"..." He still didn't respond.

He moved his body, about to give out under him, and slowly, slowly brought his upper half up.

"Why?" she cried like a lost child.

"..." He didn't know himself.

He didn't have a clue how strong Accelerator was.

He didn't have an inkling what he could do with his body this messed up.

The Imagine Breaker still slept in his right hand, though...

...and without a doubt, he possessed within him a reason for clenching that fist.

For he believed that if he could use that hand and save a girl unable to move and driven to a dead end by Accelerator, then that would be wonderful.

Thus, Kamijou arose.

He planted his own feet and no one else's onto terra firma.

"Misaka, you were originally going to Accelerator, weren't you?"

He looked at her.

It seemed like it had been such a long time since he had seen her eyes. They were beet red from weeping.

"Tell me, Misaka. Where is he about to start the experiment?"

3

Little Misaka arrived at her destination: a train switching yard.

Analogous to a garage for buses, this was where a great many trains were maintained and where the cars would go to rest after their last run for the day. The wide area was about the size of a school courtyard. One side was covered in the same sort of gravel as the kind under railroad tracks, and there were more than ten rails all lined up parallel to one another. At the end of the tracks were many sheds with large shutters, like the rental garages at a harbor. Surrounding the outside of the sorting yard sat a large quantity of metal containers used for freight trains. They were piled up like bricks, with height rivaling three-story buildings. Thanks to the cluttered mound of containers, the outskirts of the switchyard were as complicated as a three-dimensional labyrinth. If the containers were mountains, the switchyard in the middle would be a basin.

There was no sign of life in the sorting yard.

The final run for trains in Academy City was at the end of the school day, so human presence disappeared swiftly from these yards as well. The workers' lamps were off, too, and without any private homes nearby, there was no light. Despite the metropolis in which 2.3 million people lived, this place was wrapped in a darkness black enough to allow stars not normally visible to be seen when she looked up at the night sky.

At the center of this uninhabited darkness stood *something*.

The strongest esper in Academy City—Accelerator.

When Little Misaka saw him there, assimilated into the dark around them, she felt an illusion that she had been thrown into Accelerator's giant organs.

The boy of white laughed in the blackness.

That eerie pallor, like an eyeball dropped into boiling water, simmering gently.

"The time's about eight twenty-five, eh? So then, you're the dummy target for the next experiment, yeah?"

Out of Accelerator's mouth came a voice, like the white darkness had spit it out. He smiled so wide it seemed to tear his face apart.

Little Misaka didn't move an eyebrow, though, and replied, "Yes, Misaka's serial number is 10032, responds Misaka. But would it not be proper to first confirm the password just to be sure you are a participant in the experiment? suggests Misaka."

"...Tch. Throwin' off my rhythm," he spat. "Whatever. I don't got the right to say anything to someone tagging along, since this whole 'experiment' is to make me stronger. But you sure do seem calm. Don't you think about stuff in this kind of situation or anythin'?"

"I am having difficulty understanding the vague word *stuff*, answers Misaka. There are three minutes and twenty seconds remaining before the start of the experiment. Have you completed your preparations? confirms Misaka."

Accelerator narrowed his eyes ever so slightly, then bit something in his mouth in exasperation. *Chew, chew.* It looked like he was chewing on gum and drawing out its sugary flavor.

"? What are you ingesting? asks Misaka."

"Ah, a finger."

Accelerator replied casually, spitting what was in his mouth to the side like spit.

It was a crushed, saliva-covered, sloppy piece of flesh...

And yet, that thin female fingertip had barely managed to retain its form.

"I had the chance, so I figured I'd borrow one for a bit, y'know? But man, human flesh really ain't all that good or anything. I heard stuff about it having little fat and tasting sour, but this is way beyond that. When ya bite it, it feels like you're tearing apart a thin bundle of stuff. Those pigs and cows and shit that evolved for our consumption really are admirable, ain't they?"

Accelerator wiped his lips with his arm, as if removing the taste from his mouth.

However, Little Misaka moved nary a muscle at his action.

"General pork and beef are treated with phlebotomy, then seasoned with salt and spices, offers Misaka. In addition, one can observe a change in protein quality by heating it up, so a comparison to the taste of living flesh would yield an inaccurately performed experiment, would it not? suggests Misaka candidly."

"'Zat so?" responded Accelerator, peeved.

Little Misaka didn't understand why Accelerator would ask a question like that. It was true that she had frozen in fright when she spied him in front of the used bookstore, but that was because the black cat was at her feet. She feared involving entirely unrelated lives with this experiment.

"Seriously, after doing this ten thousand times, a guy gets bored, so I was just thinkin' we could kill a little time or somethin', but I guess not. You're impossible to talk to, you know that?" he said, relaxing. "You know, I don't get why you throw away your life like this. I mean, my life is the most important thing for me, and I'm always thinkin' my own body is the best. That's why there's no limit to my thirst for more power. I don't really give a damn how many hundreds or thousands of you die for it, I can just laugh it off, ya know?"

"Misaka is the one who cannot understand parts of what you say, answers Misaka. You are already the strongest Level Five in Academy City, correct? If you already stand at a place where nobody can hope to reach, you would feel no need to aim yet above that, estimates Misaka."

"The strongest, heh," answered Accelerator in an uninterested tone.

"Strongest, strongest, strongest, huh? Well, yeah, sure. I'm the strongest esper in this city, so that probably means I'm the top esper in the entire world, too."

"But, y'know," he responded, looking truly bored.

"In the end, **I'm only the strongest**. I am the strongest esper in Academy City. Hmph. So why does everyone around me know that? Frankly, it's because they actually fought Accelerator and lost, right? So in other words, **'his strength seems interestin', so let's pick a fight with him'**—that's all they think of me."

Those red eyes turned into a happy grin.

"That's no good. No good at all. What's Level Five for, then? I'm goin' beyond that. I want absolute power, so it would be ridiculous to even think of challenging me or even considering the thought of fighting me at all."

He declared that he aimed for that sort of invincibility.

The boy offering his own aspirations slowly extended his two slender arms out to either side.

His suffering right and his poisonous left.

Spreading his hands parallel to the ground, he smiled. His arms were like venomous snakes that could kill a person at a touch.

Like a holy cross spouting darkness.

"So, we good now? Just die already, you good-for-nothing manufacturing error."

However, Little Misaka didn't twitch an eyebrow at the boy grinning mockingly at her.

She simply declared indifferently with a voice like a clockwork puppet:

"Eight twenty-nine PM, forty-five seconds, forty-six, forty-seven—We shall now proceed with trial number 10032. The subject, Accelerator, should please stand by in his designated location, conveys Misaka."

Thus...

...began the unavoidable experiment at 8:30 PM sharp.

4

Having left the black cat with Mikoto for the moment, Kamijou dashed through the night streets alone.

There was a sizable industrial area on the west edge of Academy City.

Apparently, the train switchyard there was the location of the 10,032nd "trial."

"..."

He remembered hearing the number 10,032. Little Misaka· had given it as her serial number back in that alley.

Could it be..., he asked himself, urgency gripping his heart.

He needed to get to the trial area as soon as he could, but unfortunately, the buses and trains had also already returned early to their garages at the final school closing time.

With the majority of the transportation facilities asleep for the night, he had no choice but to run under his own strength.

Though he was aware his body didn't have much stamina left, he didn't have the luxury of calmly pacing. He grit his teeth, intent to run through the shopping district at full force.

Forcing his wrecked body to move, he continued his sprint, whittling down what stamina he had left (if he had any to begin with).

He made it past the shopping district and into a residential area, feeling the bustle and illumination of the city grow farther and farther away. As he hurried past them, even the student dormitories began to grow sparse. After cutting through a small wooded area that was grown artificially, he came to the industrial area.

Academy City contained many of such areas for commercializing research inventions created by its citizens. However, they were different from the backstreet workshops like the filthy rental warehouses downtown. The "manufacturing buildings" were tall but without windows, and they stretched on endlessly through the city. They were arranged into sections quite properly, but because of that, not a hint of life emanated from them. It might be faster to imagine a city made up entirely of office complexes.

There was no one in town.

The factories were set up to operate twenty-four hours, but because of the perfect soundproofing applied to them, they didn't make a peep. With this view like a dead city, Kamijou felt a chill on this midsummer's night.

Mikoto, left by herself on the iron bridge, held the frightened black cat in both arms.

Now that she thought of it, animals didn't like the electromagnetic waves unconsciously emitted from her body. But that wasn't important to remember.

"...What an idiot," she muttered to herself in the darkness.

She had wanted to stop him. At the very least, she had wanted to go with him to the test area.

But Kamijou had told her no.

What was important was that Imagine Breaker defeat Accelerator. Another Level Five being present, especially if she took Kamijou's side, would end up transforming the result into a party of people, including a Level Five, having defeated Accelerator.

He told her that if she wanted to rescue Little Misaka, then she should leave this to him.

He promised that he would come back with Little Misaka at all costs.

Mikoto stared down the bridge from which he had disappeared.

She understood it logically. She wouldn't be able to do anything if she went to the test site. In fact, she ran the risk of destroying the solution he had labored to come up with. So she needed to stay here. She got that. In a logical sense, she knew that.

But…

Something aside from logic wasn't quite as willing to understand.

Mikoto gritted her teeth.

"…Like hell I can do that, you asshole!"

She ended up chasing after Kamijou, holding the cat by the neck.

There was no way she would leave him be.

5

At 8:30 PM, the switchyard transformed into a battlefield.

The unlit area blinked with pale blue camera-like flashes.

The two pairs of footsteps belonging to Little Misaka and Accelerator pounded into the gravel.

They were separated by less than ten meters.

"Hah! Why're ya walkin' around like it's nothin'? No plan? If you wanna feel the pain that bad, then I'll make you cry! Maybe suck on a cough drop or somethin'!"

Accelerator, his arms still spread wide, crouched and closed in on Little Misaka like a wild beast.

His charge lacked the very concept of defense. It didn't even have the concept of *offense*. This was the battle of someone who reflects every attack and kills an opponent just by touching them. It was simply a matter of how quickly and certainly he could make physical contact with his opponent. That's all he needed to think about.

Since attacks would all bounce off him, there was no slowing him down. Given this outrageous mayhem, like he was a tank plunging straight into the middle of a demolition squad, Little Misaka—

"Ah?"

He let out a discontented voice. Little Misaka had taken backward steps to place distance between them, as if running away from his pursuit. To the right, then to the left; as she kept up her flight, she surveyed the situation around her. Accelerator, the carnivorous animal, truly bored, shifted his attention and was hot on her heels.

"What, what, what is this, this unsightly display? Hey, now, just what are you expecting, eh?! It doesn't matter how long you stall, a miracle ain't gonna happen!"

Little Misaka didn't listen. She continued to widen the gap between them, her enemy ever in her sight. Accelerator, whose head vessels were about to explode out of his indignation toward her halfhearted act, noticed then the air around him was tingling; it was charged.

"You're such a freakin' bore! Don't you know this ain't gonna do shit? Were you thinkin' I'd just play along with your useless resistance?! Hah, not a chance!"

Accelerator laughed scornfully. Whatever kind of attack it was, he could reflect it as soon as it made contact. In any case, Little Misaka seemed scared and wasn't firing any lightning attacks at him directly. Sparks were bursting around him, but there wasn't a single attack-like *attack* within them.

What the hell's she doin'? he thought, grinding his teeth. Then he realized that he was short of breath. He thought for a moment he'd been talking too much while he was running and used too much oxygen, but something else was up.

He smelled something. The sharp scent was ringing warning sirens.

"There's no wind tonight, I see…"

Little Misaka's voice echoed through the windless switchyard.

"…which means Misaka may have a chance at victory, says Misaka over her shoulder."

Accelerator again took in the situation around him. Little Misaka was still running away, the lightning being placed around him, the unusual shortness of breath, and himself, who would reflect every attack directed at him.

Hah. I get it. Ozone, huh?

It's possible to break apart the oxygen in the air by using an electric charge. Normally, what one calls *oxygen* is itself comprised of two oxygen atoms, but once two oxygen atoms have been split apart, they have the property of connecting three apiece into "ozone."

Oxygen and ozone are entirely different. Breathing it wouldn't fill up your lungs.

And as one can guess from its use in antibacterials and sterilizers, ozone is toxic.

There wasn't an attack that could ever get to Accelerator, but he was no different from other humans in that his body inhaled oxygen and exhaled carbon dioxide. Therefore…should the oxygen around him be utterly depleted, it would be possible to drag him into an oxygen-deprived state.

There was no need for Little Misaka to draw close to him. Instead, she got as far away from him as possible and continued to steal the oxygen from positions where his attacks wouldn't hit her—that was the important part.

"All right, all right! You're the freakin' best, you know that?! I take it back, you really *are* tryin' to be a worthy opponent! Ha-ha, this ain't boring at all! Ten thousand of you were killed, why not bring out a crafty trick like this! Is that it?!"

Accelerator stuck to his pursuit, smiling gleefully. He was positively beaming, even though he was the one being driven back.

"How-ev-er. There's a weak spot!"

Little Misaka's shoulders suddenly gave a twitch and trembled for a second, and he continued:

"If I catch you, then your plan is a failure!!"

His advancing foot suddenly caused the gravel behind him to explode. He probably altered his foot's direction. As if he had fired rocket engines on his heels, he took merely one step and closed the seven meters with the speed of a bullet. Shocked, Little Misaka attempted to jump backward—but Accelerator charged right up to her much more quickly and ruthlessly than she could act.

"Hey, you're really gonna die if you're not dodgin' this shit with all you got!"

The left hand he thrust forward as he shouted gently stroked her cheek...However, when his hand touched, Little Misaka's neck gave a most disagreeable *snap*. Her vision spun, her body rotated like a bamboo-copter, and she came down hard onto the gravel below.

And yet he had taken it easy on her.

If he had really wanted to kill her, her body would have exploded the moment he touched her skin.

"Okay, then! Got a question for ya. How many freakin' times have you died already?!"

With his broken laughter, Accelerator resembled an all-encroaching darkness.

His smile ripped across his face, broadening, filling her view.

Mouth opened wide enough that drool might fall out, he flung a jeer at her.

Everything from this point on was Accelerator having free rein. Taking advantage of the opening in her defense, he shoved the toe of his shoe into her curled-up body and threw a fist at her arched back to stop it from moving. He made each blow only strong enough to break her body and not kill her. She plunged into a whirlpool of pain comparable to being thrown into an oil drum, which was then struck by a metal baseball bat many times over.

"Gh...fuh...?!"

Even rounding her back now a challenge, Little Misaka lost out to the force of the kicks jutting into her gut and flopped on the ground faceup. Blood was flowing over one eye, blocking its sight; had her forehead been cut? Her vision grew vague and blurry as Accelerator took a rough breath. He was wiping saliva trickling from that slicing smile with one of his hands.

After all of that, Little Misaka still held no resentment toward him. It wasn't that she couldn't hate him if she wanted to; it was just that she hadn't ever learned the value of her own life. The experiment, which used one 180,000 yen Little Misaka life, would end, and her remains would be collected and disposed of like a frog after dissection.

That was all.

It should have been it.

And yet, Accelerator jerked to a halt, having noticed something. He slowly craned his neck to look over his shoulder and behind him.

What...is...?

Accelerator's body stood as a wall directly in front of the prone Misaka's position, so she couldn't tell what he had spotted. However, he was frozen in place, as if he had managed to somehow forget that this was the all-important experiment to elevate his status from "the strongest" to "invincible."

"...Hey. What happens to the experiment now?" he asked abruptly, still unmoving.

Hazily, she thought his question rather out of place, having asked the person he was trying to kill. Though she waited, Accelerator didn't budge from that position.

She crawled along the gravel and followed his gaze.

There, she saw a civilian—one who had no connection to the experiment.

There stood Touma Kamijou.

Accelerator probably didn't know what the manual had to say on civilians interfering with the experiment. He stared at the newly arrived high school student with an uncertain look, and then:

"...Get away from her, you bastard."

Kamijou spoke as if stabbing those words into Accelerator.

A fury that seemed almost shocking to the touch engulfed his body.

"I said, get the hell away from Little Misaka this instant. Are you deaf?"

Accelerator's face bunched up in a scowl at that. Then he finally turned back to her. Giving her a somewhat reproachful, red gaze, he asked:

"You. Misaka's the name of your model, that right? So what, does this guy know you or somethin'? Hey, look, I'm beggin' ya, don't drag unrelated civilians into the test area!"

His face looked like he had lost interest in something.

"...Seriously now, work with me here. So what do I do? Should I go and make sure the guy never speaks of the secrets of this experiment again, or what? Damn, that'll leave a shitty taste in my mouth. I mean, he's not some disposable puppet like you, he's a real-life—"

"I said, stop your fucking babbling and get the hell away from her, you piece of garbage!!"

The thunderbolt of Kamijou's bellow stopped Accelerator's words in their tracks.

Accelerator stared at him. He couldn't believe his eyes.

He stared like a child who had never been scolded once since birth.

"Who do you think you are? You got no idea who you're pissin' off here. You're callin' *me* a piece of garbage? I'm one a the only seven Level Fives in this city, and they even say I'm way above all of *them*, and you're callin' *me* a piece of garbage?! What are you, God? Don't make me laugh."

His low, quiet, bloodthirsty voice seeping with static electricity escaped into the air around them.

It was as if his tremendous malice converted all of the night's blackness into millions of eyeballs, and they all stared Kamijou down.

"..."

However, the boy still stared back at him.

His scorching eyes silently said that he didn't care whether his enemy was the strongest, or highest, or best, or whatever.

"...Heh. That's interesting..."

Accelerator's red pupils froze.

There was a difference between being "the strongest" and being "invincible." "Invincible" refers to when the battle is decided before it even starts, whereas "the strongest" is only decided after actually fighting.

In other words...

Accelerator being the strongest meant only that people wanted to pick fights with him just to see—

"—You're pretty funny, you know that?"

His focus shifted away from Misaka and settled on Kamijou, meaning that he was leaving this experiment to the side for the moment; crushing Kamijou was a hundred times more important to him.

The eyes of the boy of white contained a crimson, bestial enthusiasm.

His grin was thin and broad—slashing across his face like a knife through melted cheese.

"..."

However, Kamijou didn't take a single step away.

His foot took another step forward.

"What..."

Little Misaka couldn't believe what she was seeing.

That boy was about to attempt combat with Accelerator. This was someone who could defeat entire armies with a smirk on his face. He didn't even have weapons.

That boy said this to Accelerator.

He demanded he get away from Little Misaka immediately.

That meant that his reason for showing up at this battlefield...

His reason for putting his life on the line...

"...are you doing? Misaka begins to ask," she stammered, her voice shaking.

"...O-oh, it's the little sister. But man, you two really look alike. Do you even weigh the same as her?"

She didn't give a thought to how greatly her worthless self would die in this "experiment."

"...Heya. Thanks for the stuff with the juice and the fleas yesterday."

But he wasn't at all part of this, nor could he be reproduced en masse.

"...*Oh right, a name! This is your cat, so take responsibility and name it, all right?*"

Could she let even one normal person in the world be hurt because of this experiment—

What is...this...

Something inside her was stinging with pain.

Try as she might, she couldn't figure out what it was or why it was there.

...Misaka bears doubts as to her own state of mind.

Despite that, Kamijou kept his mouth shut and took yet another step into the battle zone.

Little Misaka forced her thoughts to a halt and began to implore him to stop.

"What are you doing? asks Misaka a second time. You are irreplaceable, yet you are here for an imitation that can be created however many times is needed. What on earth are you doing? asks Misaka a third and final time."

Her logic was consistent. Her tone was undisturbed. What she said seemed measured. It appeared to have come from her programming. This led her to conclude that her mental state was all green.

In spite of that, her heart was beating out of control. Her breath was unbelievably shallow—she tried again and again to breathe, but she couldn't capture any oxygen.

Little Misaka wanted to stop that boy from entering the test area.

Little Misaka wanted to prevent that boy from clashing with Accelerator.

But her useless, messed-up body wouldn't move normally, so still lying on the gravel, she continued to plead with him to stop him from entering.

She did not realize that her words were his very impetus.

"Misaka can be automatically manufactured at the press of a button, so long as the required materials and medicines are procured, explains Misaka. A borrowed mind in an artificial body. My retail price is 180,000 yen. Why would you stop the entire experiment just to save the 9,968 remaining in the inventory—"

"…Shut up," the boy cut her off.

"Wha…t?" Little Misaka asked in return.

"I said shut up, got it? None of that matters. Artificial bodies, borrowed minds. Automatically producing more at the press of a button given the necessary equipment and drugs. Your price being 180,000 yen. I don't give a damn about any of that! Words like that don't mean a damn thing!"

The boy roared with a fiery anger, as if howling at the night sky.

And yet his voice was pitiful, as if being struck with cold raindrops.

"I'm standing here to save you! I'm fighting to rescue you and not anybody else! So spare me the artificial body, borrowed mind, being produced automatically at the press of a button, retail price bullshit!"

Little Misaka failed to understand.

She didn't comprehend what this boy was trying to say. It wasn't like she had lied. She could, in fact, be automatically produced as many times as needed at the push of a button. If they were missing one, they could replenish their numbers with another, and if they needed twenty thousand, they could just add twenty thousand more. That was all she really was, wasn't she?

"—There's only one of *you* in the world, moron! It's so simple, and yet you don't get it!"

But for some reason, the boy's roaring voice, powerful enough that she thought he might cough up blood, reached her.

She hadn't believed him or anything.

Little Misaka still thought losing her life wouldn't be a problem.

But here, in front of her, was someone yelling that he didn't want to lose someone so insignificant.

The boy probably had no powers of his own.

He didn't possess anything that would cause him to be called the strongest in Academy City, either.

"Don't go dying on me. I've still got a million complaints for you—"

And yet, Little Misaka thought that this boy was *strong*.

"—so I'm going to go ahead and save you now. Shut up and watch from there."

She had been *able* to think that his way of life made him stronger than anyone else.

6

He may have been the *strongest*, but Accelerator was not invincible.

As long as his was an abnormal power, Kamijou's Imagine Breaker would shatter it with a mere caress, even if it was a miracle from God. Accelerator's "reflection" might be an unbreakable defense capable of bouncing back a nuclear explosion, but it wouldn't protect him from at least Kamijou's right hand.

Whether or not he was the strongest, able to take on the entire world against him...

...if it wasn't impenetrable enough to defend against his one and only Imagine Breaker...

...then there was sure to be a chance at victory hiding within that margin of error.

"..."

Kamijou checked his surroundings.

All around him, in an area approximately one hundred meters in diameter, the ground was covered with gravel and steel rails. The two of them stood on this level playing field, nowhere to hide. Ten meters separated them. If he ran with all he had, he could bridge that distance in just three or four steps.

He stopped breathing.

Then he lowered his body slightly like a spring.

"Oh...woooohhhhhhh!"

With Accelerator dead in his sights, he exploded into a sprint.

His opponent, however, didn't make a move. And he didn't even make a fist; both hands were still dangling at his sides, he wasn't properly calculating his center of balance. With a smile that seemed to melt through his face, he...

Step.

As if tapping to a beat, Accelerator lightly touched the gravel with the sole of one foot.

Roar!!

In that moment, the gravel underfoot erupted as if he had stepped on a land mine.

The cloud of gravel scattered in all directions, bringing to mind a shotgun going off at point-blank range.

"...!"

By the time Kamijou realized it, it was too late.

As soon as he raised his arms to protect himself, at least a dozen pebbles, both big and small, crashed into his body with a dull, loud *wham!* The overwhelming impact gently lifted his legs off the ground. Before he knew it, he'd been blown backward with great force. He rolled along the ground and, after tumbling a few meters, finally drew to a stop.

"...You're slow."

As he laid there, dizzy with pain, an unpleasant voice—one like pieces of rusted metal scraping together—encroached upon his awareness.

He looked in that direction without even thinking to stand back up.

"You ain't worth my time at all. You're a hundred years too frickin' slow!"

Accelerator stomped his foot into the ground.

Somehow altering the vector of the impact, one of the steel rails sleeping at Accelerator's feet sprung upright. He punched the standing rail away with the back of his hand like one might swat away a spider.

The action was almost like giving a light knock on the head to an unreasonable child.

However, a deafening *gong!* like the sound of a church bell reverberated throughout the switchyard. The rail bent over in the middle, then flew straight for Kamijou with the force of a cannonball.

"!!"

He urgently rolled along the ground, then leaped to get out of its way.

A moment later, the squashed clod of steel plunged straight into the area he had been sleeping in, like a holy sword.

I dodged it by the skin of my teeth, thought Kamijou, when the heavy metal lump, weighing hundreds of kilograms, uplifted a storm of gravel from the impact. It looked just like a meteorite falling into the ocean.

Countless tiny stones penetrated through to his entire body.

A blow to the chest drove the oxygen from his lungs.

"Gah...hah...!"

He fell to the ground, and Accelerator sent two more rails hurling at him, then a third.

The steel anvils dancing through the air were no more avoidable than the bullets of a handgun.

If he got hit by one, he would unequivocally die. Even if he managed to slip by them, a hail of gravel would come down on him like a rain of buckshot, and over time the accumulated damage would eventually kill him.

The only thing he could do about any of this was to keep tumbling across the ground. He predicted the direction the gravel would fly in after being whipped up by the cannon shells thrusting into the ground. By jumping in the same direction, he could at least lessen the damage a little...That was virtually his only option.

He couldn't get close.

He dodged ten or twenty steel rails, bombarded by the rocks and dust all the while; as this was happening, he was being gradually led from the middle of the switchyard to its outer edges.

Even so, he considered the battlefield to be at a stalemate.

He was being one-sidedly beat up on, of course, but he believed that Accelerator had yet to be able to land a decisive blow.

However, with a *whoosh*, his line of thought was cut off by the sound of slicing wind.

"...?"

He suddenly leaped backward, thinking a rail was flying at him... so he could kill the impact of the shotgun blast of gravel as much as he could. Despite that being his intention, however, the metal pillar, for some reason, never came.

Still on his guard, Kamijou knitted his brows dubiously...

...as a steel rail whipped right over his head and stabbed into the ground behind him.

"?!"

At the time, he had already jumped backward to dampen the blow.

The rain of gravel assailed him from behind at zero range. It was analogous to a truck driving at one hundred kilometers per hour colliding with another one going the same speed. All that damage he had ended up increasing slammed into his back. Winded as if someone had hit him with a baseball bat as hard as they could, Kamijou clumsily crumpled to the ground.

Whoosh-whoosh, came the sound of the night air slicing apart.

Kamijou raised his head to see many steel rails falling from the sky.

Wha...?

He immediately tried to roll to avoid them, but the rails simultaneously hit the ground in all four directions. Huge clusters of gravel rushed toward him. It was almost like getting ganged up on by five or six guys.

He couldn't defend nor could he evade in this case. His options gone, more than a hundred of the shots stabbed into him from head to toe, limbs jerking about like a beached lobster.

"Guh...geh...agh...! Hah...hah...!"

Nevertheless, he grabbed onto one of the rails sticking out of the ground and leveraged it to pull himself back up to his feet. It certainly didn't help that his legs were shaking badly because of all the hits he took from Mikoto's lightning earlier. It also didn't do him any good for his mouth to be awash with the taste of blood.

As his consciousness hung on for dear life, he saw it.

Far in front of him. It was Accelerator, lowering himself as if his body were one giant compressing spring.

"Aha! See, you're slow, slow, slow, way too slow! You're just actin' like some pig askin' to be eaten! Step it up and act like a fox, and gimme a little bit of fun, you piece of garbage!",

There were thirty meters currently dividing them.

Without any regard to that fact, Accelerator strode over the distance with just two steps.

The gravel at his feet came up like a rocket. He closed the distance with the same sort of movements as a rock skipping across water. With incredible speed, he came into melee range with Kamijou.

A tinge of nervousness sunk into him somewhere around his stomach.

He instantly tried to stick out his arm, but Accelerator's foot hit the ground before that.

A steel rail lying under him bounded up into the air like a pogo stick. The bolts attached to the crossties started popping out like buttons on a shirt.

Before Kamijou even had time to be startled, the rail performed an uppercut and slammed into Kamijou's jaw.

"Gh, goh…!"

His body snapped up into the air. His feet were twenty centimeters off the ground. Accelerator watched him with satisfaction, and then, setting his sights on Kamijou's floating, now-undefended torso, he opened the fingers of his right hand like the claws of a demon.

That hand, which had fired a rail at him like a comet with a single, gentle stroke.

"_____!!"

The instant he saw Accelerator's right hand coming at him, in the manner of a venomous cobra, he thrust out his own right hand, even though he was still hovering in the air. Somehow, someway, his hand batted away Accelerator's, as if to prove to him that there was, in fact, a silver lining.

And with that insignificant action…

…Accelerator gave him a look of utter disbelief…

…and stomped hard on the earth as if to drive the concern from his mind.

A ground slam.

The lethal gravel that burst upward battered the uplifted Kamijou all over. His breath left him, and then he fell onto the ground, limp as a corpse. He rolled over and over for several meters with his limbs outstretched. Then, with a *thump*, his back hit something, and he finally managed to stop.

"...?"

It was the wall of containers.

Mountainous piles of storage containers enclosed the switchyard. Accelerator and Little Misaka had been right in the middle of the area, but it seemed that he'd retreated dozens of meters during his continuous dodging.

The heaps were five or six boxes high, boasting roughly the height of a three-story building.

He gave a glance to the wall of containers his back was up against, but...

"Hey, you looked away, didn't you, you moron! If you wanna die *that* badly, I'll mess up your corpse so splendidly it'll be put in *Guinness*!!"

Mad laughter.

Kamijou turned back around in a hurry. Accelerator had just lowered his body slightly and kicked hard off the ground a few meters away, leaping up into the air. It was only a standing jump, and yet his slim form instantly reached an apex of four meters.

Aimed straight at Kamijou's head was a flying kick with all his opponent's weight behind it.

He immediately rolled to the side to dodge, and Accelerator's leg collided with the metal wall of containers he had been up against a moment ago.

Boom!! came a deafening sound like a church bell.

Suddenly, the mountain of containers came crashing down.

He had essentially pulled the bottom brick out of a stack of building blocks.

Accelerator's flying kick squashed the bottom level of containers like a paper carton. Immediately, the containers on the upper levels above them rocked back and forth, then came tumbling down. Not only did *they* come down—they brought the blocks adjacent to them into the fold as well, and the entire ridge of containers fell apart like a house of cards.

Kamijou caught his breath and looked above him.

The crates, spinning toward him like giant dice, were hurtling through the air. They were about to sprinkle the ground with a heavy rain.

"!"

He immediately got to his feet. He just about jumped to the side and out of the way of the approaching boxes, but before that, he caught something out of the corner of his eye.

It was Accelerator, hunching down like a coiling snake.

In that startled moment, his opponent shot toward him, fast as a bullet, as if trying to chase him down as he fled from the containers.

A deluge of containers, each weighing more than a ton, was nothing someone who could reflect any forces needed to worry about evading.

Kamijou, however, was a different story.

If he tried to dodge the container above him, he wouldn't be able to dodge Accelerator's pursuit…

…but if he tried to intercept Accelerator with his right hand, he'd be squashed by the container.

"…!"

He didn't waste any time. He kicked the gravel at his feet up toward the closing enemy.

Of course, that didn't make him stop.

"Ha-ha! You think that'll work or somethin'? If you're gonna do somethin'…then at least make it good!!"

The swarm of gravel collided with Accelerator's body. When it did, the barrage altered its trajectory, ricocheting straight back at Kamijou even faster than he had sent them.

He immediately crossed his arms in front of him to protect his face and chest.

Not a moment later, the cluster of pebbles assailed him with the force of a shotgun, striking him all over his body. He was blown a few meters backward as if he really *had* been blasted with a cannonball.

Thus he avoided the containers overhead...

...as well as placed distance between him and the incoming Accelerator.

"Aah?"

Accelerator gave a groan that almost sounded like admiration, and immediately after, the containers all collided with him. A huge gravelly fog flew into the air, and all the dust obscured Kamijou's vision. Then a stampede of containers came cutting through the cloud, one-sidedly rolling toward him with intent to kill. They danced around with the unpredictability of dice inside a cup and raged about like they possessed sentience.

Damn it...!

Kamijou made a last-ditch effort, jumping to the side to flee from the bounding boxes.

For the moment, the crates stopped, but the dust they whipped up obstructed his vision. No, wait, this wasn't dust. Apparently there had been flour or something inside the containers. He found himself unable to see more than a foot in front of him with the powdery mist.

It was a white, 360-degree curtain surrounding him.

He didn't know when or where Accelerator would come diving through it to attack him. A hopeless anxiety settled within him. It felt like he'd been thrown into a wild beast's cage blindfolded.

Contrary to his expectations, he heard a voice coming from the white fog in front of him.

As if to purposely call attention to his own position.

"Hmph. Looks like there was some flour in those containers. There ain't any wind today; it feels good, but you know, this could kind of be a dangerous situation, eh?"

"?" Kamijou dubiously watched for his opponent to come out at him, but...

"Well, you know how accidental explosions happen in mines and stuff, right? They're not because they were messin' around with explosives or anything." His playful voice gave away the grin on his face. "I hear it's actually 'cos **the fine particles from the shaved-down rocks and stuff inside the mine get all in the air. Just like now.**" ·

Kamijou's shoulders jerked.

He suddenly realized what Accelerator was trying to do, and he immediately tried to drag his mangled body away from it.

"I'm told that the powder floats into the air, and then there's a spark. Somethin' about the speed of oxygen combustion going through the freakin' roof. In the end, the air itself just turns into one huge bomb supposedly."

Kamijou was no longer listening.

Without sparing another glance, he ran on to get away from there as soon as possible.

His back turned to Accelerator, he fled from the giant space covered in powder.

He ran, ran, and ran some more.

Then Accelerator's voice dug right into his spine.

"Hey. You've at least heard of dust explosions, eh?"

Just then, all noise was deadened.

The very area throughout which the flour particles had spread, thirty meters in diameter, had turned into a giant bomb. It was as if gasoline in a gaseous state had been ignited—the air all around him exploded into a whirlwind of flame and burning winds.

It was then that Kamijou just barely made it out from the misty curtain.

The wave of impact struck him in the back and flung his body down onto the gravel, but at least he had managed to avoid being caught in the fire.

However, the difference between a dust explosion and a normal one is the way in which it burns through the oxygen in the air. This explosion sucked up all of the oxygen around him in the blink of an eye, dramatically lowering the air pressure.

Fortunately, they were out in the open, not a confined space, so it wasn't enough to create a vacuum. However, the dramatic change in pressure squeezed his insides tightly. Of course, had this been a vacuum, his body would have exploded.

"Gah...hah...!"

Kamijou barely managed to move his wounded body and stagger to his feet. The switchyard had lit up like afternoon thanks to the sea of flames. He turned back to look toward where the containers he'd fled from had been.

Accelerator was walking toward him.

Calmly, he trod closer, amid the crimson purgatory he himself had created.

"Man, oh, man. Oh, right. Didn't I just go through this before? It's tough even for me if there ain't any oxygen. Ah, thought I'd die there for a sec. You might be the first person in the world to get me to a spot where I thought I'd die. At least you can be happy about that, right?"

His singsong voice really did sound like he was just making small talk.

"Ku-ku. I wonder if that rules out the whole tagline they slap on me? You know, about it being A-OK to shoot a nuke at me? Well, actually, I guess I'd just hafta bring along an oxygen tank. Hey, if I recall, there was a kind the size of a hair-spray bottle, eh? Any idea how much those can do?"

Witnessing the boy persisting in his lighthearted conversation despite walking within the hellfire caused terror to seize Kamijou's heart.

"...!"

He immediately tried to take up a fighting stance.

However, the damage had already permeated down to his legs. They were trembling badly.

"...So? What're ya gettin' ready for anyway?" asked Accelerator, within the flames, tilting his head like an innocent kid. "You can pull out all the stops, but you won't get a step closer. And even if ya did get close to me, what could you do then, huh?" He spread his arms wide refreshingly in the inferno. "Anything that touches my body has its vector changed. Even your blood flow counts, got it? So if you ever accidentally touch me, that's it. All of your arteries and organs will explode and you'll die for good. Ya dig?"

"…"

Kamijou stopped his legs from shaking.

Even if his right hand *could* break through Accelerator's reflection…

What could he do after that?

The only part of him that could touch the guy was his right hand, so he was essentially boxing with the other behind his back. And even if his hand *did* make it to Accelerator's face, if he grabbed onto his arm just once before he could pull it back, then it would be…

However, Accelerator grinned amiably at the frozen Kamijou.

"Well. It's not like you have to worry about it that much. I mean, I actually think you tried pretty damn hard, you know? The fact that you're still breathing against the great Accelerator by itself is a freakin' miracle. It'd be sorta greedy to ask any more, you know?"

He smiled at him in a good-natured way in the middle of this duel to the death.

"Lord, man. Good thing your potential is so low. My reflection won't work as well if you're *that* weak! Man, you saw right through to my, whaddayacallit, *vulnerability*. If you were one of those stupid strong Judgment members or one of them Anti-Skills carrying some high-tech weapons with 'em, I woulda reflected their first attack and that woulda been it."

Accelerator applauded him, standing in that blazing ocean.

And then, in a voice that sounded sincerely comforting and appreciative…

"Ya did good. Ya did real good…So just rest now."

His body sank down low through the flames.

Roar! The pale boy sprinted at Kamijou with the speed of a bullet, dispersing even the sea of fire in the process. Though there were dozens of meters between them, he brought it to nothing within

two or three steps. He slid right up to Kamijou like a rock skipping across water.

"…!"

A jolt of tension crawled from his stomach up to the tip of his nose.

His suffering right and his poisonous left.

Those hands could alter the vector of anything they touched, and they were simultaneously hands of darkness able to grant a permanent end to any living creature. For example, a simple stroke of the skin would allow him to reverse the flow of blood in his veins or the direction of the bioelectric field around his body—either way, the person's heart would explode.

Accelerator put his hands together.

His pair of palms, linked as if bound by handcuffs, thrust fiercely toward Kamijou's face.

He instantly tried to move back, but his trembling legs were snarled. Moving them properly was something he couldn't do.

Those hands of his approached his face, ready to crush his very soul.

"Damn it…aaaaaaaaahhhhhhhhhh!"

He reflexively shut his eyes, then swung out his right hand in the knowledge that his desperate act would fail. He threw his right hand out in front after depriving himself of his vision, without knowing what he was even aiming for…

…*Thud.* With some kind of dull sensation, it punched Accelerator's face away.

"Eh?"

If anything, at first, Kamijou was more surprised at his strike than Accelerator was at being stricken. He never thought it would hit him. And he was under the impression that even if it *did* connect, such a bloodied, weak fist wouldn't actually do any harm.

However, it blew Accelerator backward and he fell onto the gravel and writhed.

"Ah-ha? That…hurt. Ha-ha. What was that? Interesting. Ha-ha-ha, damn it. Great, that's the best! You really did a wonderful number on me, you know that?!"

The pale boy crouched on the ground, like a demon about to hatch from an egg, and laughed with wild enthusiasm.

However, Kamijou wasn't listening to him.

Now that he thought of it, something had been weird since the start.

He'd battled with Accelerator this far, so why hadn't he realized it yet?

There was an overwhelming handicap separating the two of them. Accelerator could kill someone just by touching them. On the other side of things, Kamijou would die instantly if he touched him with anything but his right hand.

To top it all off, the damage he'd taken from Mikoto's lightning attacks still lingered in him, and he wasn't in a state to move his legs properly.

And yet…Even though he was fighting with such a handicap…

…Wait…

Accelerator came right up close to him.

That right hand of his, which could kill a person with a touch, flew straight at his face.

…Wait, is he…

Kamijou avoided it just by bending his neck to the side.

He didn't have any kind of training in the army or anything, but avoiding it came easily to him.

Could he be…

He balled his right hand into a fist.

Then he stepped in even closer to Accelerator, who had missed his attack, to land a counter.

Could he actually be…a total weakling?

"Gbah?!"

Kamijou's fist struck Accelerator square in the face. Accelerator's hands, moving at him in a knifelike, complicated pattern, failed to so much as nick Kamijou's skin. Weaving around his two cobra-like arms, Kamijou placed a third fist right smack in Accelerator's face again.

"Damn it, what is this? What the hell's with the way you're movin'?! Quit zigging and zagging like that! What are you, a freakin' eel?!"

Accelerator made an attempt to latch on to the fist retreating from his face, but Kamijou's hand slithered back out too smoothly.

"Hah, you've never lost, huh?" Kamijou taunted, dancing to and fro. "That's **exactly** why you're weak! You can beat anyone with one hit, and you can reflect any attack with ease. Someone like that would never know how to brawl!"

Yes—the difference between the two of them came down to that.

Accelerator didn't *battle* with anyone—he one-sidedly *murdered* them. And because the ability his body had was altogether too strong, he never needed to learn how to fight for real.

Looking at him now, Kamijou could see that Accelerator's stance was a mess. He wasn't making fists; his open hands pretty much announced that he would be jamming his fingers at him. He also wasn't giving any thought to the way he carried himself or to his center of gravity.

But that's just how powerful Accelerator's ability was—worrying about any of that had never been a necessity.

He was able to insta-kill every enemy who presented himself, so he never had to practice techniques to skillfully defeat enemies.

He was able to reflect any attack, so he also never had to put in the effort to try and read through those attacks and dodge or block them.

Technique and effort—they are, essentially, the means granted to the weak to compensate for their lack of strength.

However, Accelerator's "strength" was no more than that of his ability. It wasn't his own strength.

What if there were a right hand that could render the one-trick pony useless?

The opponent was not some invincible enemy whom he could never defeat no matter how hard he tried.

If he was only the *strongest*—an enemy who was simply difficult to beat—then…

Kamijou's chance at victory lied within that ever-so-slight gap between being *invincible* and being the *strongest*.

"Tch…You're gonna regret runnin' your mouth like that, you piece of garbage!"

Accelerator lightly tapped the ground with one foot.

A steel rail sleeping underfoot bounced up like a kangaroo.

The steel cannonball would make it to Kamijou's body if he could just pummel him away with it.

However, Kamijou didn't allow that.

Predicting his attack, he moved to intercept it, bringing his right fist into Accelerator's face again. As his body slammed into the ground and tumbled away, he manipulated the "direction" of the gravel splashing up in his wake and fired off a huge shotgun blast at Kamijou's upper body.

It didn't connect.

It was such a telegraphed attack. All he needed to do to evade it was drop to the ground like he was going to start crawling.

It wasn't as if Kamijou was an especially good fighter.

Even against common thugs, he could only win one-on-one; if it was against two, then it was dangerous; and three meant he was getting the hell out of there. That was the extent of his skill.

Despite that, Accelerator didn't reach him.

Kamijou's own thrown punches didn't have the weight of his body behind them. They were more like jabs in boxing. They were only to gauge the enemy. More power was used to pull his arm back than to thrust it forward.

However, despite that, Accelerator took them like he was being hit by a truck.

The fact that Accelerator had never been defeated also meant that he had never really fought before. His ability had always been so strong that he didn't have a chance to utilize regular exercise abilities. Kamijou couldn't earn crushing victories in altercations with street punks, but he was more than able to deliver the smack-down to this homebody who'd never fought anyone in his life.

Accelerator, having taken a handful of quick rights to the face, reached out his hand recklessly and shouted.

"…! Kh-hah, how interesting. What the hell is that right hand?!"

The strongest of them all, who hadn't a loss to his name…

And the weakest of them all, who refused to give up no matter how much he lost.

As to the question of which was stronger, the verdict here would go to Kamijou. If he lost one hundred times, he'd get back up a hundred times. If he lost one thousand times, he'd crawl back to his feet one thousand times. Those losses converted into power, and that power slammed a right fist into Accelerator's nose.

Until now, he had reflected every single attack coming at him. Even if he understood that a blow would present a threat, those thoughts wouldn't be connected to any reflex to avoid it. He didn't pay attention to the blows to the face; he only recklessly followed the fleeing Kamijou while waving his arms around. It looked for all the world like a small child being lovingly teased by an adult.

Accelerator himself was the one who understood this the best, and he couldn't stand it.

His pride as the strongest in Academy City was teetering over the ravine between it and reality with scraping noises.

Scritch-scratch. An unfamiliar pain that seemed about to crush his nose chipped away at Accelerator's concentration even further.

"Damn. Damn! Damn it!!"

There was an explosion at the howling Accelerator's feet. His body leaped toward Kamijou like a bullet. The impact of the soles of his feet kicking off the ground—by optimizing the kinetic energy therein that would have otherwise dispersed, he quickened his movement speed by two times normal, or maybe even three.

However.

"What is this, damn it? Why can't I hit you one fucking time?!"

Despite his carnivorous velocity, he couldn't reach Kamijou.

It didn't matter how much speed he achieved. As long as his aim was obvious, it was easily avoided. A knife can be used to kill someone, but if a kindergartener is the one holding it, it doesn't present a threat.

The fight had been virtually decided already. The injuries from Kamijou's small punches had piled up by now, and they had drained the energy from the legs of the strongest and **wimpiest** esper of Academy City.

Right when the strength left Accelerator's knees with a *crack*...

Crunch! Kamijou's fist rammed into Accelerator's face with the full power he hadn't used until now.

He hit him like a golf club whacking a ball. By twisting his waist and using it as leverage, Kamijou's one hit knocked Accelerator off his feet and sent him rolling to the ground beneath.

"Hah...hah...?!"

Accelerator sat up and looked in front of him. After confirming Touma Kamijou wandering toward him, he used his hand to push himself backward.

It hurts.

For someone who had automatically reflected any attack that came at him, it was an unfamiliar sensation. To him, all pain spots were simply sensors that transmitted pleasure from his skin to his brain. His infantile nervous system had a complete lack of resistance to "pain," and such intense stimuli made it feel about to burn out.

"...Those Sisters were all living in the best way they could, too."

Kamijou gripped his right hand.

"They tried their hardest to keep on living, and they put so much work into it...," he said, clenching his teeth. "...So why the hell does someone like you have to devour them all?!"

Accelerator's movements froze in pure terror.

But Kamijou didn't stop.

Accelerator shook his head as if to say, "Please, no." He didn't know what losing was like. He had never lost before—not once in his whole life. He hadn't a shred of tolerance to losing. Of course not.

Until this very moment, he'd been someone no one had ever even *considered* could be defeated.

However, Kamijou still didn't stop.

The night wind teased his bangs, which swayed like a nameless flower blooming in a graveyard.

...Wind?

Suddenly, as Kamijou, the look of the devil on his face, drew closer, Accelerator noticed something.

Wind.

"Kuh…" Accelerator grinned. Kamijou stopped in spite of himself. Perhaps he got the sense of some indescribable danger. Accelerator didn't worry about it. Now that he had realized it, it was too late.

"Kuka…" His power was to change the direction of anything he touched. Momentum, heat, electrical current. No matter what force it was, if it had a vector, he could manipulate all of it. That's all his power was.

"Kukaki…"

Then in the same way…

If his hand could catch the direction of the wind current in the atmosphere…

Then it was possible to grasp the entirety of the gargantuan wind movements flowing in every corner of the world…!

"Kukakikekokakakikukekikikokakakikukokokukekekekokiku kakukekekokakukekikakokekikikukukukikikakikukokukukeku kakikukokekukekukikukikokikakaka…!!"

Accelerator reached up with his hand as if to grab the invisible moon.

Roar!! came the sound of the wind swirling.

The boy in front of him blanched. It was too late for him to realize it now. An enormous atmospheric vortex, like a hole opened in the earth, was already above his head, taking on the form of a sphere and waiting there to be launched. The gravel around him danced into the air with *click*s and *clack*s, and the huge whirlwind of destruction, dozens of meters around, uttered the delighted cry of a newborn.

Smiling, Accelerator called, "Kill him."

The wrecking ball made of the world's atmosphere cut through the wind…

And the 120-meter-per-second maelstrom, spinning fast enough to fling cars out of the way, morphed into a howling lance and easily flew toward the boy as if directed by a giant's hand.

7

Sound, wind, and air all deadened.

Accelerator beheld the terrible spectacle he had created. The gravel, which had once been covering the switchyard, was being ripped into the air by the mass of wind. It would hide one area from vision, then reveal another, many times over. The boy was blown backward a good twenty meters and had crashed into the support pillar of wind generator back-first. He was leaning against it, crumpled on the ground. It might have been more pleasant for him had he fallen onto the gravel. Either way, the end result would be the same. Ramming wind at 120 meters per second into something was not too different from a car running into something during a traffic accident, no brakes.

In reality, Kamijou wasn't budging an inch. Beneath that pillar, his limbs were sprawled out. Accelerator saw him and doubted whether he was even still alive.

"…Hmph."

For something he'd thought of by chance, this had been stronger than he'd predicted.

But it was still incomplete. Unlike his automatic reflection capabilities, altering the direction of something by his own volition required him, of course, to consider both its original direction and that which he wished to change it into.

The wind—more accurately, the flow of air—is described by complex equations that involve chaos theory. Without using the Tree Diagram, no one could get close to an accurate prediction.

He didn't think that he, just one person, had calculated the flow of all the air in the atmosphere in his head.

What he just did took everything he had. He only manipulated the wind in Academy City here and there.

But still, this power...He didn't need the strength of a Level Six anymore. If he could determine the wind flow more perfectly and more accurately, then he could obtain a might capable of destroying the planet itself.

The whole world was in his hands.

A feeling of elation surged through Accelerator's body. He only felt the triumphant sensation rising in his throat so vividly because he'd been driven to the brink of defeat.

He was sure of it again.

Nothing existed in this world with the ability to stop him.

Whether it be a nuclear bomb or a strange right hand, *nothing* could prove to be an obstacle to him.

"Ku..." Accelerator finally started to laugh. "What in God's name was that?! You talked real big, but when it came to it, you were all bark! Now get back up like a cool loser should so I can smash you again!"

He howled above, spreading his arms as if to embrace the night sky.

"Compressing the air...compressing...compress. Hah, I get it. Yeah, I thought of something *real* good. Hey, stand up, 'weakest.' It won't be worth it unless you stick with me for a while longer!"

Kamijou didn't reply.

Dozens of steel rails stuck out of the ground, like crosses marking graves. In the midst of it, only raging gales and mad laughter blew through this cemetery like a wind of death.

The black cat at Mikoto's feet meowed unhappily.

Mikoto Misaka took that moment to set foot into the switchyard.

She had been watching Kamijou's battle since its inception. Time and time again, she had wanted to intervene, but doing that would mean this plan would fail. Until this very second, she could do nothing but watch silently as Kamijou was beaten further and further to a pulp.

She was at her limit.

If she let that boy fight for any longer, he really would die.

"Stop right there, Accelerator!"

From dozens of meters away, Mikoto stuck out her hand. It was already gripping a coin placed atop her thumb. Purple sparks poured from her body. All she had to do was give a light flick of her thumb to fire it at three times the speed of sound, the skill that had earned her the nickname Railgun.

But Accelerator didn't even turn to look.

The violent winds increased in intensity as if to challenge her.

If she made an attack, its full force would bounce right back.

Bombard him with one powerful strike and that impact would fly straight back at her.

"…"

Her fingers trembled.

If a Railgun were reflected, it would blow her to pieces at thrice the speed of sound.

Odds were 185 to 1 that in a battle between Railgun and Accelerator, Mikoto Misaka would be brutally killed. The result of that calculation, spit out by a cold machine, unalterable, stabbed icicles into her heart.

Despite that, she raised her eyes.

You don't want to protect somebody because you know you could defeat their enemies.

You fight enemies you know you can't beat *because* you want to protect someone.

"…op, Misaka."

Just then, she heard her name being called.

It was a very weak voice, but one belonging to a boy she knew well.

"…Stop, Misaka!"

Mikoto's hand paused at Touma Kamijou's cry of agony.

In Kamijou's plan, if Imagine Breaker, an Impotent, didn't defeat Accelerator, a Superpower, then they couldn't fool the scientists.

That strategy would fail at the moment Mikoto raised a hand to interfere.

If Mikoto didn't interfere, the storm system would annihilate Kamijou's body...

...And if she did, it would mean Kamijou would have let ten thousand Sisters die.

"..."

Nevertheless, she couldn't stand by and watch.

Of course she didn't want to let the Sisters be killed.

She had one more method to use. If she lost to Accelerator on purpose, the scientists might be tricked and stop the experiment.

She didn't want to die.

In the end, though, it mattered not how much she struggled. There had never been any other options available to her from the start.

"...I'm sorry."

That's why she took this last chance to apologize to Kamijou.

None of the choices she could make would be able to save him. Letting him be crushed by the maelstrom was out of the question, and Kamijou wouldn't be able to endure it if he let the Sisters die *or* if Mikoto died alone to stop it.

He desired a conclusion where he wouldn't lose anyone, he wouldn't lose anything, and everyone would go home happy. She apologized because she was about to blast that dream to kingdom come.

"So I'm sorry..."

She apologized in a singsong voice for being so selfish.

"...But I still think I want you to live."

Kamijou shouted at her to stop.

He stretched out with one hand that would never reach her, desperately trying to stop her, despite being so beaten up he could no longer stand.

Mikoto smiled softly.

He didn't realize it—it was because he was here to say it that she was able to overcome her fear of death.

"_____

_____"

She pointed her right hand at Accelerator, the enemy she would never defeat.

If she used her magnetic rail and popped the coin, there would be no going back. Accelerator wouldn't take any damage because of his omnipotent reflection, but she should still be able to avoid the death that would approach her afterward.

I wonder why it had to turn out this way, she thought vaguely.

Why can't there be another ending? A totally different one, a better one, where everyone can smile? The one everyone wants? Why can't there be a conclusion where no one has to die, no one has to lose anything, and everyone can smile and go back home?

Mikoto's thoughts hung idly in the air, and as if to mock them, Accelerator spread his arms and stared up into the night sky. Suddenly, all the wind floating through the city focused on one single point about a hundred meters above his head. As soon as a violent storm gathered there, a brilliant white light appeared, like the kind a welding torch might emit.

Plasma.

When air is compressed, it takes on heat; internal combustion engines use this principle. All the air in the city had been shrunk at an extremely high rate of compression, transformed into a superheated ball more than ten thousand degrees Celsius, forcing the atoms in the air nearby to break into cations and electrons, then completing its metamorphosis into a high-energy plasmatic state.

The single point of light sucked in air and immediately swelled to twenty meters in diameter.

The brilliant white glow utterly conquered the darkness surrounding them.

Waves from the searing heat caused a burning pain on her skin.

"_____!"

Mikoto's spine cried out to her as if she were just paralyzed.

A human could no longer defend against a strike like that. The storm of high heat was enough to uproot a nuclear shelter right out of the ground; even *thinking* about opposing it nakedly was ridiculous.

In the category of lightning users, Mikoto Misaka was without a doubt the strongest in Academy City.

Since plasma is atoms that have split into cations and electrons, then she might be able to return them to atoms by placing the electrons back into the cations.

But what would come of that?

Even if she reverted the plasma back to its original state, Accelerator would just collect more wind and re-create it. It would be no use to try electric attacks, either. Preventing this onslaught would require someone who could manipulate the wind like he was doing now. It goes without saying that while Mikoto could use lightning, she had no way to control wind. She gritted her teeth as the reality of her powerlessness dawned on her, and—

—then, she realized something simple: The important thing was that if she could manipulate the wind, she could stop Accelerator.

"Ah." Mikoto hung her mouth open like an idiot.

Clatter-clatter. The wind generator's propellers were making a sound like a laughing skull as they spun.

That plasma was something created from compressing the wind gathered from throughout the city. It was nothing compared to using the entire world's wind, so that meant there must be some limitation on his ability. For example, perhaps he needed to calculate the wind's original and desired vectors in order to control them of his own will, unlike his simple "reflection."

Then she should mess with the wind in the city, thus messing with his calculations.

There were many wind generators all over Academy City. There were more than 100,000 of them, weren't there?

Also, by infusing the propellers with specific electromagnetic waves, one could get them to start turning.

Even if each single propeller only created a miniscule breeze, more than 100,000 of them churning the air was a different story. It might be enough to cause Accelerator to release his control on the wind.

But it wouldn't mean anything if Mikoto, a Level Five, were to manipulate the propellers.

In this battle, she couldn't directly intervene or stop the experiment.

If she were obeying the condition that she would not use her own ability to interfere with this fight, then technically…

This was a job for Little Misaka and for no one else in the world.

Little Misaka's and Mikoto's power were on different levels. Little Misaka's "Radio Noise," a watered-down version of Mikoto's ability, could only be called Level Two at most. Given the amount of propellers they needed to get moving, she wasn't worth much.

However, there were ten thousand Sisters about the city.

And unlike Accelerator, doing all of the wind flow calculations by himself, the ten thousand Sisters could link their brains via their brain waves and predict the wind flow in unison. Just like the Tree Diagram had done with its superefficient parallel processing.

Little Misaka's broken body didn't seem to still have the strength for her to get up onto her feet again by herself. She hesitated to demand yet another reckless thing of her.

But it was the only thing she could do.

"Please, get up. I know I'm asking a lot, and I know how cruel what I'm saying is to you. But please, just once, get up!"

But asking was all she could do.

"There's something I want you to do. No, there's something that only you can do!"

No one losing anyone or anything…

Smiling together and going home together…for that…

"Just once! Please hear me out! I can't protect you all. No matter how much I struggle and strive for it, I could never protect you! So please, please!"

One where everyone is smiling, the one everyone wants…

To arrive at the happiest conclusion…for that…

"Please, use your strength to protect his dream!"

*   *   *

Little Misaka, her consciousness cutting in and out intermittently, certainly heard the original's cry.

What she said was indeed absurd, she thought. If she was going to crack the whip and force Little Misaka to use her ability, even though her heart seemed about to stop, then why couldn't she just use her own, which was many times superior? Hazily she wondered, but didn't understand it.

However, she couldn't complain.

The original's words were unreasonably violent, but...

For some reason, Little Misaka saw in her a child on the verge of crying, begging for help.

"..."

Little Misaka had never discovered any worth in her life.

Her mind was empty, injected with a program, and placed into a body of flesh reproducible at the push of a button. She seriously believed that she was easily replaceable should her 180,000 yen life be destroyed.

Unfortunately, she thought, *But I still don't want to.*

Her life didn't actually have any value, but now that she knew that there were people who would feel sadness over losing such a paltry thing, she could no longer die.

And she was *able* to think that if her paltry existence was able to help the girl on the verge of tears, then, well, that would be a wonderful thing.

There was something she had to do.

She had found something she needed to protect.

"There's something I want you to do. No, there's something that only you can do!"

I find it difficult to understand the meaning in what she says—

Slowly, Little Misaka began to direct strength to her limbs.

—but somehow, it has given me quite the surprise, thinks Misaka, noting her candid feelings.

It was because there was someone to say that to her...

...that she was able to stand once more.

8

Roar! The wind moaned, and the spherical mass of plasma floating overhead collapsed.

"Wha...?"

Accelerator looked up automatically. The energy had been drawn from wind all over the city and squeezed tightly enough into one point to create plasma. The wind had shifted. It was only for a moment, but it definitely changed. The event had introduced an error into the air's rate of compression and had caused the plasma to flicker.

Did I mess up the calculation? he thought, rebuilding the equations anew. It was a pain; unlike his simple reflection, actual *control* necessitated that he calculate both the vector before it changes and the one after.

That said, it only took ten seconds for Accelerator to perfectly adjust this enormous calculation. This level of thought wasn't a problem for someone whose brain had been developed. Ability Development was a part of the teaching methods of Academy City. In other words, the strongest esper equated to the *smartest* esper.

However...

As if to escape from the equations assembled by his perfect mind, the stream of wind in the city suddenly changed its movement. It wasn't a coincidence; it was almost like the wind itself had a will and was slipping through the gaps in his calculations.

The mass of compressed air above him started to disperse, and the plasma began to melt away into the air.

What? What the hell's this?! My calculations are free from error! And besides, these irregular squid movements can't possibly be from natural wind!

Could he truly be unlucky enough for an actual wind user to be using their power somewhere in the city? No, this irregular air flow was permeating every corner of the city. If there *was* a wind user with the abilities to outpace his own calculations, they would have to be a designated Level Five. But as far as he knew, there were no espers like that among the seven Superpowers.

Then what the hell..., he thought, panicked, when he picked up a dry *clatter-clatter* sound.

It was the sound of the propellers on the wind turbines turning.

Wa...it. Yeah, I heard of this. They got some electric dynamo motor, and you can get it to spin if you fire some microwaves at it...!

Accelerator turned back to the Sister, whom he should have beaten down already.

However, he didn't see a girl on her deathbed.

The person who was there was his enemy.

That...bastard...!

Accelerator's red eyes shifted into a murderous scarlet.

Even if his control over the plasma and the raging winds had been hijacked, the Sisters were no threat to him. The only thing on the planet that could penetrate his flawless defenses was that right hand.

"I'll kill you."

Accelerator took a step toward the Sister, a skin-splitting smile coming onto his face.

Then Mikoto Misaka stepped between the two of them.

"...Think I'll let you?"

Mikoto's voice was quiet enough compared to the raging vortex that the air might have swallowed it completely. But for some reason, it plunged straight into his eardrums.

"Hah. Don't push your luck, you low level. You can't reach me. You can't even slow me down. Eye exams only go up to twenty over ten, right? Same thing. The highest level in Academy City's Five, so I'm actually just *putting up* with it here."

Mikoto didn't respond with anything. She probably understood that fact the best. She was standing here and now because she *still* didn't want to run away.

Accelerator decided she was in the way, so he figured he'd go ahead and kill her first, then—

*　　*　　*

Rustle. He heard the sound of something from behind him.

"..."

Accelerator slowly turned around.

There before him, he saw the unbelievable. The boy, the one who got blown back by 120-meter-per-second wind and crashed into the support beam of a wind generator, was slowly getting back to his feet.

There were too many wounds on the boy's body to count. It also seemed like blood was spurting from the wounds whenever he as much as nudged a nearby muscle. He couldn't channel much power into his body, both his legs quaked, and both his arms hung lazily at his sides like the branches of a willow.

And yet he still wouldn't stay down.

No matter what.

"..
....Tsk!"

The moisture fled from Accelerator's throat, leaving it as dry as a desert.

Looking at him sensibly, it was clear that boy couldn't fight anymore. A person who had sustained that kind of critical damage should be easy prey for Accelerator to smash.

If he didn't want to fight face on, he could always kill Mikoto and the Sister, then retake his control over the gales and plasma. He was standing a lot closer to them than he was to the boy, after all.

His logic sung a sweet tune to him: that he could win with ease if he dealt with them calmly.

However, something else in him dreaded showing his back to *that*.

Every corner of his body grated with blaring warning signals.

If he were a normal person, he would have realized that it was the fear of pain and dealt with it.

"You're damn interesting..."

Accelerator clenched his fists.

"...You're the most interesting thing I've ever met, ya know that?!"

Kamijou brought his smashed-up body one step forward.

He felt like all his blood would turn to steam from the smallest of movements. He felt like his consciousness would run away from the most miniscule of thoughts.

In spite of that, he advanced.

Within such a haze, he didn't have a proper grasp of the situation. Why was all this violent wind blowing? Why had the plasma disappeared? By what logic had he survived? His mind was in such a desolate state that his mind had left such important things by the wayside.

But there was just one thing.

Directly in front of him, he saw Accelerator trying to kill Little Misaka.

He saw Mikoto step between them to act as her shield.

And that was all he needed to know.

That was more than enough reason for him to get up again.

"You're damn interesting..."

He heard Accelerator's voice.

"...You're the most interesting thing I've ever met, ya know that?!"

As he howled this into the night sky, he clenched a fist and dashed toward him with intent to kill. He closed the distance in the blink of an eye, like he was shot out of a cannon, using that power of his to change the direction of his feet's force as they kicked off the ground. *Convenient*, thought Kamijou. There was nothing better than for Accelerator to come to him. Given his battered body, he would probably have collapsed before getting to him.

Touma Kamijou had no strength.

The strength to stand on his feet and walk. The strength to form words with his tongue. The strength to have thoughts in his head.

His body had not even the tiny amount of vitality required for any of these.

However, he gripped his right hand.

Into a fist.

And brought his eyes up.

Accelerator flew straight up to Touma Kamijou at the speed of a racing bullet.

His suffering right and his poisonous left.

Those hands of his, either of which would kill a man with just a touch, approached Kamijou's face.

For a moment, time seemed to stop.

Pouring all the power remaining in his body, which was as minute as strained lees, Kamijou swung his head down and ducked. The suffering right passed through empty space above him, and he batted away the follow-up from the poisonous left.

"Grit your teeth, 'strongest'...," said Kamijou to Accelerator, whose heart had frozen, his two-part killing blow nullified.

At super-close range, near enough to touch, he grinned like a savage beast.

"...My 'weakest' attack is gonna hurt a bit!"

Then...

Touma Kamijou's right fist plowed into Accelerator's face.

His slender, pale body slammed down into the gravel, and he tumbled away with his arms and legs violently flailing.

EPILOGUE
Only One
ID_Not_Found

When Kamijou opened his eyes, he was in a dark hospital room.

There was a strange sensation around the area of his lips, possibly because of anesthetics. He looked around without moving his head. It was the same old private room, and it seemed to be the middle of the night. The only sound in the quiet room was the weak noise of the air conditioner. When he noticed the lack of a change of clothes or any fruit, he deduced that not much time had passed since he was brought here. After all, the only person in the room was Little Misaka, quietly sitting on a chair at the side of the bed—

"Yes?!"

He nearly jumped out of the bed in surprise, but his anesthetized body refused to budge.

Little Misaka's usual form was dotted with bandage wrappings. That was all well and good, but then he heard a black cat meow. He wasn't able to see it from this angle. It must have been curled up underneath the bed.

Lastly, he noticed Little Misaka's hands embracing one of his.

It didn't *really* matter, but she was holding both her hands to her chest, and Kamijou's own had been brought to the boundary between possibly touching her breasts and not touching them.

"Mi-Mi-Mi-Mi-Mi-Mi-Misaka…? Huh? That's odd, how come

I'm experiencing such a happy event? I don't remember anything about having triggered those sorts of flags!"

The black cat under the bed, startled at his shout, let out a shriek.

"...Your words are as incoherent as ever. Just to make things clear, you were the one who grabbed my hand, says Misaka in easy-to-understand modern lettering."

"That's a lie! I can't possibly be so unfulfilled that I would grab a girl's chest after nearly dying while under the effects of full-body anesthetics! It's a liieee!"

He lamented and wanted to bury his face in his hands, but of course, his body wouldn't be moving any time soon.

Little Misaka gave an impassive "?" expression, and after witnessing his disgraceful conduct, she spoke.

"You only went so far as to grab Misaka's hand, explains Misaka helpfully. It was Misaka's own intention to bring your hand to this position, so I do not believe that any fault lies with you, she answers."

"...Princess. Mayhap you might inform me of the reason you did such a thing?"

"I was simply measuring your brain waves and pulse rate via your bioelectric field, responds Misaka. There is no particular sexual meaning included."

Se—?! Kamijou thought he would stop breathing, but suddenly he realized something.

Huh? Wait, so that means it is touching? My hand is touching it now? You know, I can't feel anything because of the anesthetics! Agh, damn it, I can't even move a finger, either! Damn iiiiittttt!

"D-damn it...What amazingly rotten luck...!!"

"Odd, I do not detect any abnormalities in your speech center, says Misaka, offering reasons as to her unease."

Little Misaka looked stoic as usual.

The black cat under the bed mewed sleepily.

Kamijou gave up on his useless effort and looked back at Little Misaka.

"Well, we both got out of that somehow, huh?" he said, sort of poking fun at it, but there was definitely something welling up inside him. Actually, he'd be worried if there wasn't—he wouldn't know why the hell he'd risked his life like that in that case.

"In regards to that, answers Misaka," she said, petting the cat. "Misaka cannot return to the same world as you yet, she declares straightly."

Kamijou's shoulders twitched. Was the experiment still going on?

"No, nothing like that. It appears to have been decided that the experiment would be phased out along with the defeat of Accelerator, reports Misaka kindly and thoroughly." She paused for a moment. "The problem Misaka has right now is the issue with Misaka's body, explains Misaka."

"Body?"

"Yes. I am originally a clone created from Big Sister's somatic cells, and my body was stimulated to grow extremely quickly through the administration of various drugs, explains Misaka. A clone already has a short life span, and in doing so, it is decreased even further, says Misaka, asking if you understand."

"..."

He was at a loss for words.

Because that was just too much. Everyone had combined their strength and pulled her out of hell, and yet her time to live was limited to begin with, and whatever choices she made and however she proceeded, she could never be together with everyone?

She had still fought without voicing a single word of complaint...

And now, no matter how hard she tried, she had nothing left in her hands.

"So I will temporarily go back to the research institute and undergo adjustments to this body...Are you listening? asks Misaka, glaring at you."

"Huh? Adjustments?"

"Yes. By adjusting the hormone balance that originally stimulated my quick growth, and by tuning the rate of cell reproduction in the cell nucleus, it is possible to recover a certain amount of life, responds Misaka...Hello? You hadn't translated that to mean that the story was over, did you? demands Misaka."

"Those adjustments…They'll make you better?"

"…I seem to detect an implication that you don't believe it *can* make me better, says Misaka, growing irritated."

Then the black cat under the bed meowed.

Little Misaka gathered up the slightly frightened thing, then headed for the door with an "Excuse me."

"Ah, wait. You're leaving already?"

"It's all right," she replied without turning around. "We will be able to meet soon, asserts Misaka."

"I see," he said, closing his eyes.

That was fine. Leaving some kind of special promise would make it feel like they'd never meet again. If they could see each other soon—if she really believed that—then the most serious words of parting were the ones said normally.

The story hadn't ended here.

They would go on until one day, today's events would be an insignificant memory.

He heard the door shut through the darkness of his closed eyes.

Medicine-induced sleepiness washed over him.

But still, Kamijou smiled, dreaming of the day they would surely meet again.

When he next awakened, dawn had already broke in the hospital room.

"Oh, you're awake?"

Mikoto Misaka was the one saying that. Her face was thickly colored with exhaustion, but she still managed a smile.

"Here you go, I brought you a cookie as a present. I picked out one of the kind of expensive ones in the basement of the department store, so it's probably pretty good. At least, I think? Make sure you tell me how it is. If it's bad then I'm never going to that shop again."

"Mm. Homemade cookies really are the best."

"…What kind of character were you expecting me to be exactly?"

"No, well. You know, like the clumsy character trying so hard in her own clumsy way and making a messed-up cookie?"

"Again, what the hell were you expecting?!"

Kamijou and Mikoto spent their time bickering like they usually did. He was happy that they were standing in the normal world, having a normal time.

"Oh, right. Little Misaka came by in the middle of the night."

He told her about what had happened the night before. About how Little Misaka would go back to another research agency for a while so they could fix up her body and how she promised to come back to Kamijou again.

"Uh-huh."

That's all she said.

She narrowed her eyes like she was watching over something important, but at the same time, there was a shadow somewhere in her face.

Mikoto was indeed able to stop the experiment.

And she was able to save the lives of close to ten thousand Sisters.

However, she couldn't save the other ones.

Because of the DNA map she had carelessly provided, twenty thousand Sisters had been born just to be killed. That fact was probably something that would weigh on Mikoto's back for the rest of her life. Even if no one blamed her for it, even if everyone in the world forgave her, she would carry that burden as long as she lived.

"But, you know," Kamijou said. Mikoto quieted and looked at him.

Her eyes looked like those of a child left alone in an unfamiliar city. He couldn't bear to look at them.

"If you hadn't given them your DNA map, none of the Sisters would have been born in the first place. There was definitely a lot of messed-up stuff with that experiment, but I think you should be proud that at least the Sisters were given life."

Mikoto was silent for a while.

Finally, she said, in a voice like a child about to cry:

"...Even though more than ten thousand of them got killed because of me?"

Kamijou answered with affirmation.

Saying that something is hard. Thinking that something is painful. Those simple things that anyone can do are still things they couldn't do if they weren't born.

"So the Sisters don't hate you or anything. That experiment was screwed up all over, but I think they still thanked you at least for the fact they were born despite that."

Mikoto gulped at what he said.

Seeing her with that expression made his face smile a little through the anesthesia.

"So you can smile. The Sisters definitely aren't wanting you to be down in the dumps all by yourself. The Sisters you wanted to protect aren't so petty as to be satisfied with shoving the pain of their own wounds onto someone else, right?"

The next time he opened his eyes was for his three o'clock snack.

However, he couldn't eat the cookie Mikoto had given him.

The reason for this was because Index was glaring right at him as he laid on the bed, peering into his eyes from super-close range.

"Touma, don't you have something to say?"

"..

.....................Umm, good morning?"

That immediately got the top of his sleepy head bitten. His body jolted up in the bed as if her teeth had been a stun gun. Just how far would she go to be satisfied? Just ask the shriek that his mouth unleashed like a cat whose tail was stepped on.

"Wait! Wait a second! I'm hurt too much this time for jokes and stuff, okay?! Besides, why don't you act a little like a housewife and worry about me some—"

"I did worry about you!" Index cried, cutting him off.

He unintentionally sucked in his breath at her voice. She sounded like a spiteful child.

"...I did...worry about you," she repeated once more.

She released her teeth from Kamijou's head, then wrapped her arms around it like she was hugging a pillow.

Kamijou thought for a moment.

If their positions were reversed, what would *he* have thought?

If Index had gone off by herself while he wasn't looking, did some crazy stuff, then got carried to the hospital. How much would *he* blame himself for not talking to her about it, staying in his own little carefree world?

Kamijou gave a single "sorry."

Index replied that it was okay, then released her arms from his head and smiled.

That was the decisive difference between the two of them.

She was the kind of person who was able to laugh here instead of getting one-sidedly mad at him.

"Anyway, you faced a problem by yourself, again, again, again. If you don't wise up and talk to me a little about it, I might actually have to seriously lecture you, I think."

Kamijou gave a hearty laugh to evade her.

When it came down to it, he *was* still hiding his amnesia, too, after all.

She sighed. "Well, it won't do any good to say much further, so it's okay. In the end, what were you fighting for, Touma?"

Kamijou gave a "hmm?" to confirm what she said once, then answered.

"For myself, of course."

Just like that, his normal daily life began anew today.

Touma Kamijou would walk the same path he always did, without turning to gaze back on the past.

Whether or not his path led to a combined dream with Little Misaka didn't matter to him.

Whatever the case, he just wanted there to be a future so happy it would even surprise Little Misaka upon their reunion.

AFTERWORD

For those of you who have bought this book from the start, it's a pleasure to see you again.

For those of you who just bought the three volumes all at once to read this, it's a pleasure to meet you, and thank you very much.

I'm Kazuma Kamachi.

...Uhh, this book *is* called *A Certain **Magical Index***. Yes, now that you have finished reading the book, you may hold your gut and laugh uproariously. Has there ever been such spectacular (and meaningless) trickery? I'm not sure. For those of you who dive into the afterword first without a care, please try giving the book a read. Everything will become clear then.

But before you throw the book across the room, just hear me out. The truth is that this book does touch on magic in a few places. One of them goes without saying—the scene Index is in—but there are passages here and there explaining the architecture of magic.

This method, where magic is the theme and yet the word *magic* is never stated, is apparently called "everyday magic." It's mainly used in children's literature, but I decided to give it a test run here. It would be a greater blessing than I deserve if you read this book in turn with a friend and start discussing where and how many magic conversations are hidden and things of that nature.

To tell you the truth, I'm sort of a rule junkie—I'm a huge fan of hidden rules that aren't directly related to the story itself but are actually slipped in here and there.

If you want an everyday example of what I mean, there're the ISBN codes.

On the back cover of this book, there should be the letters ISBN and a series of numbers following it. Even if you know that they're indicating something about the brand name, I don't think there are many people who seriously consider the meaning of those numbers.

If we give one a look, my own work *A Certain Magical Index, Vol. 1* is 4-8402-2658-X. There's no way to know what this is all about from just this, so let's compare it to another work. Suzu Suzuki's *A Rabbit by the Waterside* is **4-8402-26**31-8. Huh. That 4-8402-26 is also in Hazuki Minase's debut work, which was the same month as mine, *The Barrier Master's Fugue*, which is 4-8402-2659-8. And when we compare it to my 4-8402-2658-X, it's only one number off!

So now I would think, perhaps the 4-8402-26 indicates Dengeki Bunkou, and the numbers after that go in order of publication. However, Tooru Hayama's *9S Volume 1* is 4-8402-**24**61-7. Huh? Given the above numbers, it should be a 26 there.

Investigating further, we find that Kyouichirou Takahata's *HHO (01-03)* is 4-8402-**24**14-5. It's still 24. These two books with the 24 there were released in 2003, and the other works with the 26 were released in 2004. Thinking about it that way, those two digits might represent the year.

The reason for the leap from 24 to 26 in the span of one year is probably that the following two digits are the number of released titles. If we assume Dengeki Bunkou releases ten books in a single month, then the number of books released in a year comes out to be between one to two hundred. The 24 skipping to 26 is probably to leave a buffer should the number of released titles go into the triple digits.

…I thought up to this point thus far brimming with confidence, but more than likely, it isn't correct. Rather, there's a high probability that I'm way off the mark and don't realize it. But for me, what's important isn't finding the correct answer, but rather enjoying imagining all sorts of rules, so I'm okay with that.

For all those who read the above, ended up getting interested in this and looking at the back cover, I recommend figuring out the numbers that represent the JAN code. It seems that there are some fixed rules hiding in that as well, so maybe you can kill some time with it.

Now then, the rule that this inferior Kamachi is wondering about is the Dengeki Bunkou spine. Apparently its color depends on which author wrote it. What could the color separation rule be?

One: It's a measured choice based on color psychology.

Two: It's a rotation of colors in order of debut work.

Three: It depends on the editor's mood.

After mulling it over, I'm secretly thinking option two, but what do you all think?

A great thank you to my supervisor, Ms. Miki, and my illustrator, Mr. Kiyotaka Haimura. The ones who granted me this poor work riddled with more holes than a beehive are those two for sure. By myself I'm more like a small bird whose wings were plucked, so let's please remain on good terms with each other from here on out.

And a huge thanks to you, who picked up this book. I'm doubtlessly only where I am today because of you.

Now then, praying that this book will forever remain on your shelf, and wishing that it leaves a vivid impression on your memory, today, I rest my pen down here.

Twenty thousand Sisters...did I slip a world record in here?

Kazuma Kamachi